TIME IN DUST

SINDHANA

ISBN 979-8-88704-994-6

*To all grandparents of the
past, present, and future...*

Time in Dust

Fate decides to play a terrible game with Akshara. She is forced to meet Haasini under the most challenging circumstances. The first world war is raging like wildfire in a demon's cove but love too is blooming in the most romantic form when young Haasini meets Aadhi. Their sweet dreams are only beginning to come true when he is shipped off to war-infested Europe.

As Akshara discovers the dark truth of Haasini's love story, she is faced with a couple of harsh choices in a world she knows nothing about. She must choose wisely, for only one of them can help her stay alive.

Contents

The Great War

5th February, 1916
Downtown Trichinopoly, Tamil Nadu

They lay still in bed, trying to fathom the depth of the situation they faced. Haasini's hands hugged her chest while she stared at the wooden roof above. Aadhi keenly observed her actions and decided to lighten the mood. He turned on his side and gently slipped his hand around her waist. "Remember our wedding night?"

She nuzzled up closer to him. "You mean the night we spent away from each other? How could I forget something so romantic?" Her sweet voice had a great deal of sarcasm in it.

"All thanks to your granduncle."

They recounted the events of a silly, happy past and remembered the old man who gave them such a tough time. He had asked them to stay away from each other until Mercury's transit over the moon was complete. This, he believed would help them make a lot of babies later.

"But wait. We kissed, didn't we?" Haasini's eyes were wide with mischief. "You never gave me enough credit for the stunt I pulled off that night. It was three a.m. and the wedding guests were sleeping all over the floor. I had tiptoed to the other side of the house just to see you..." She gently squeezed his lower lip between her thumb and index finger. Her breath was heavy with excitement.

Aadhi rolled over and pulled her closer to him. Her heaving bosom brushed his forearm every few seconds. Unable to hold back any further, he pressed his body against hers and kissed her tender lips.

Their hands fumbled as they tried to find each other under their loose nightclothes. Aadhi managed to reach her slender waist that usually quivered even to the slightest touch. As he continued to kiss her, he tasted a trickle of something salty reaching up to the corner of his mouth while Haasini's whole body started to shiver with soft, gentle spasms. He immediately broke away only to find his beloved wife sobbing inconsolably.

"Haasini, my love! Did I hurt you?" Aadhi's face was ripe with guilt. His lips went dry and he had no clue how he messed it all up.

She covered her face with the sleeves of her blue nightdress and sobbed with even greater intensity. "Promise me..." tears choked her sentence midway. She cried a bit more before mustering up enough energy to speak again. "Promise me you will come back to kiss me again."

Earlier that evening...

Haasini walked into the well-furnished study, holding a copy of the local evening-daily, *Trichy Herald*. Aadhi was standing by the window and was lost in the emptiness of the streets outside. The war was testing the limits of a deeply wounded Indian society and he was plagued by guilt. He managed his estate and lived with his beloved wife in the comfort of their home while his compatriots fought selflessly. They chose to fight not just in India for freedom from the British, but also in East Africa and Europe, alongside the British. The nation had become a land of paradoxes.

Aadhi felt that it was high time he made his fair share of contributions. And the phone call he received earlier that day could help him change things for good.

He was pulled away from the harsh realities of war when Haasini gently wrapped her arms around his neck and planted a kiss on his right cheek. As he pulled away, she noticed the creases above his eyebrows and knew something was up at once.

"Everything okay, Aadhi?"

One look at her young, beautiful face was all he needed to feel better. He was tempted to hug her tight but decided against it. Such a burst of emotion was bound to make her feel so much more anxious than she already was.

He sat her down on the chair and knelt on the floor, meeting her intense gaze. With his hands resting on her knees, he took a deep breath and spoke in a calm, composed voice, "The great war is no longer an affair of the West and our people have been extremely generous in providing men khaki and oil. It would be a shame if we end up losing just because a few more men could not be sourced. Britain has promised independence if we continue to extend our support and cooperation."

Haasini held her breath as she knew what was coming. The reality of war had reached home quicker than she ever imagined. Her hands trembled in fear of what was ahead.

"Two days ago, I spoke to Henley and expressed interest in joining the forces. He called back this morning. Said he pulled some strings and managed to enlist me as an Officer. I will have to leave for Bombay in three days."

A man like Aadhi could be instrumental in leading his fellowmen and Henley was well aware of this fact. He also knew that close-quarter combat occurred way more frequently at the war front than most men thought and Aadhi's mastery over *Silambam* was an added advantage. He was to be directly inducted as a Commissioned Officer. It did seem like a fair deal. He had earlier donated three wagons, four horses, and two thousand rupees to the warriors' welfare fund. Under normal circumstances, it would take at least a decade of service to become a Commissioned Officer. But this was war and men were in short supply.

Aadhi opened his mouth to speak further but felt a sudden tight grip around his right wrist. A rebellious stream of tears rolled down Haasini's cheek. Her face turned pale while her lungs fought for more air. Aadhi rushed to the kitchen to get her some water.

It wasn't until after the evening sun vanished at the horizon that they managed to speak again.

"I am sorry." Aadhi did not dare look at her. "It certainly was selfish of me to decide everything on my own."

"But why them? When you are done fighting and when they have sucked up every ounce of your energy, your dear Henley would not think twice before throwing you over to the enemy," she said. Her whole body quivered as her sobs became louder.

He got up and engulfed his wife in a tight hug. "Don't you worry, *Ponnu.* I will be fine."

Young Love

22nd September, 1914

The shopping streets of downtown Trichy were bustling with activity. Haasini's mustard yellow sari added an extra pop of colour to the lively bazaar. Two other young women accompanied her and together they were attracting the attention of other fellow shoppers. Their sense of dressing was immaculate. The rich pastel shades of their youthful saris were not a common sight in this part of the city. It was mostly frequented by the older folks looking for cheap goods. The girls drew even more attention with their happy chatter and confident gait. Haasini and her cousins were determined to make the best of their visit to Trichy. It was their first time in this historic city, thanks to their older cousin Velan's five-day wedding celebrations.

"Look at those bangles!" Nandhini was ecstatic. She was the youngest of the three women and had another year before she could take her pre-university examinations.

"Come on, now! We must run or that girl will hoard the whole market and we would still be catching up with her."

Haasini and Vedavalli had a tough time keeping up with Nandini. She was already exploring the neatly stacked rows of colourful bangles made of coconut shells and glass. The salesman of one of the shops greeted the trio with his missing front teeth and a warm smile. He was dressed in a simple *veshti*. The women responded with wide-eyed excitement and went straight into the shopping mission. After a thorough scanning and selection exercise that went on for a good twenty minutes, they presented the shopkeeper with a big bunch and enquired, *"Evvalavu aachu, Ayya?"*

"One bag of cloves," he replied.

The girls thought they misheard him and enquired again, "How much, Sir?"

"It's worth a bag of cloves," he repeated. Looking at their confused faces, he added, "A bag of chillies will also do."

That was when they realized that this was a barter market. No wonder all the other buyers carried jute bags filled with spices and essentials that they would eventually exchange for the goods on sale.

Haasini tried to enquire if he would take money instead. "Would you be accepting money, *Ayya*? We can give you a quarter *Anna* or more if you insist." She motioned towards a mound of bangles they intended to take home.

"Sorry, *Thayi*. All shops in this market only accept barter payments. Even if you give me money, grocery stores will be closed by the time I get back home." he explained.

The three of them got into a serious debate on whether to give up on the shopping or to go over to a grocery store that was three streets away. That way, they could buy foodstuff and exchange it back here at the bazaar.

Their discussion was interrupted by the voice of a young man who seemed to have appeared out of nowhere. He was engaging the shopkeeper in a lively conversation. Dressed in a crisp white *veshti* and a plain indigo half-sleeved shirt, his well-built musculature demanded the attention of everyone around.

The girls were disappointed and made up their minds to go back home, empty-handed. But they were in for a pleasant surprise when the older man's voice interrupted their thoughts.

"*Ayya* here insists that you should take these for free." He packed the bangles in a yellow jute bag and handed it to them with a broad smile.

Haasini turned to look at the young man who wanted to commit to such a deal despite being a complete stranger. "Hello, sir," she addressed him and said, "This is very generous of you but we will have to decline the offer."

"Sorry, Miss. I am being rude. Let me introduce myself. I am Aadhisankaran. You may call me Aa-Aadhi," he stammered and incessantly fidgeted with the fingers of his left hand. Nandini and Vedavalli giggled as they drew wicked pleasure from watching this handsome man fumble. Haasini tried to shush them, rather unsuccessfully.

Aadhi spoke again, a bit more confident this time. "I am the organizer of this bazaar. Well, actually it was my father who started it in the first place. Often artisans in and around this area have a tough time exchanging money for goods. They are either turned down, owing to British monopoly and social class or they find no means to reach the grocers that do cater to their needs."

He paused and glanced at the young women, just to make sure that he was not boring them with his uncalled-for speech. To his relief, they seemed quite interested in all he had to say.

Nandini leapt into the conversation and enquired, "Do you own this bazaar?"

"No, Miss, I don't. As the head of the Trichinopoly farmers' guild, I am just a facilitator. You see, the farmers who don't produce enough to put up their stock for major sale have partnered with the artisans here and exchange their farm produce for this beautiful array of everyday items."

Haasini was impressed. "This is such a noble approach towards encouraging a healthy local market space. It truly is wonderful." Her smile gave away her genuine appreciation. "You are far too kind but we really cannot accept your generosity, especially, now that we know why this shopping street exists." She looked at her cousins and they nodded in agreement.

"Don't you worry, Miss. I shall be giving him half a bag of rice before he leaves tonight." Everything he said leapt straight out of his heart. "Please consider this a gift from us. I presume your contingent is new to the city." He picked up the bag and handed it to Haasini. "Welcome to Trichy."

Haasini froze and was rendered speechless by a strange feeling that made her heart beat faster than it usually did. Nandhini noticed the obvious lack of action from her older cousin and graciously accepted the gift. "Thank you!"

Mama-Machan

18th April, 1915
Madurai

With only a month left before the wedding, the world around Aadhi and Haasini changed faster than usual. Relatives, family, and friends visited their homes almost every evening. The men got busy with event management while the womenfolk took charge of people management.

Aadhi, however, was cool as a cucumber and set off to sneak a few sweet moments with his ladylove. The whole idea of the visit was concocted the day before when he was still in bed. His mother walked into his room with a hot cup of ginger tea. It was still early in the morning and the sun had only half risen.

She ruffled his perfectly trimmed hair and enquired, "All okay, *Thangam*?"

"Yes Amma, all is well. I just could not sleep until late last night."

"Talk about being in love and getting married..."

He kept his smile under wraps but not for long. His flushed cheeks and pursed lips gave it all away.

"So, when are you leaving for Madurai?" she spoke in an all-knowing motherly tone.

Aadhi was pleasantly surprised. "Madurai?"

"To meet her...you think I wouldn't know?"

Simultaneous laughter filled the room.

"In an hour or two mostly. I plan to stay at Raja's place for the night." His earnest expression remained unaltered. "It's her birthday tomorrow."

He expected his mother to say something nice but she got up without pretext and walked out of the room. Aadhi felt as if the atmosphere had flipped upside-down. He was confused. Did he say something inappropriate? He was afraid his mother felt offended by his expressive and highly unorthodox nature. Concerned that something was wrong, he pushed the sheets to one side and swung out of his bed.

"Don't even think about it. Stay right where you are. I shall be back," he heard his mother from her room. As he stood there confused and stunned, the screechy metal door of the almirah in his parents' room was thrown open. Before he could contemplate what was going on, his mother walked in with a maroon velvet pouch. It had a white embroidered pattern in the shape of a rose in full bloom.

"Open it." Her voice was full of excitement.

A pensive Aadhi pulled its strings apart. Something glittery caught his eye. He reached in and plucked out a set of gold earrings with clear emerald drops. It looked as if the outer golden rims were balancing flirtatious drops of green sherbet.

He gasped at the sight of something so dainty and feminine. "These are beautiful, Amma."

"They will look even more beautiful on Haasini. If it weren't for your father's arthritis, he and I would not hesitate one moment to pack our bags and accompany you to Madurai. I wanted to give these to Haasini at the wedding. But tomorrow is a very special day and I want you to gift them to my daughter-in-law." She pressed her fingers against the pouch and tried her best to choke back happy tears. "My father gave them to me back when I turned fifteen. It's time to pass it on."

* * *

"Machan, all set?" Aadhi was sweating profusely.

"Yes, Mama," Raghavan replied. Although just seventeen years old, he got along really well with his soon-to-be brother-in-law. He playfully thumped his chest as if to assure Aadhi that he could trust him. "Wait here...I shall announce your arrival." With mischief in his young eyes, the boy walked away to set the ball rolling.

"You don't have to make it dramatic, Raghavan." Aadhi's heart was racing as he spoke. All he wanted was to spend a few good moments with Haasini while he took her family out for a picnic by the banks of river *Vaigai*.

Anyone entering Haasini's modest house would unsurprisingly be in awe of its simple yet captivating architecture. The main door swung open to a sloping roof section that directed bright sunlight straight towards a square verandah. Surrounding it was a slight elevation, almost like a low three-sided podium. With two rooms on either side and a kitchen on the far right, the place could make anyone feel at home. The carved rosewood pillars that went all the way up to the timber-framed outer roof enhanced its overall elegance to a whole new level.

Raghavan walked towards the verandah and found his grandaunt seated outside the storeroom. "Paati, have you seen Akka? Mama is here."

"Ask him to come inside," she replied while applying slaked lime to a fresh batch of betel leaves. Her hunched back and short stature made her look very old. Just as Raghavan smiled and signalled Aadhi to get in, the old lady changed her mind and frowned. "But why is he here? Young kids these days should learn to exhibit some self-control. The wedding is only a month away."

She mumbled a bit more before Raghavan interrupted, "Oh come on, Paati. He is family now. And just to make things clear, he wants to take us all out on a picnic." His eyes were wide with excitement.

Aadhi walked in and touched her feet. "*Vanakkam, Paati.* I hope you have been well. Apologies for showing up so suddenly...just wanted it to be a surprise."

"Very well, *Maganey*... so be it." She blessed him and looked away without another word.

"Please take a seat. I'll go check on Akka." Raghavan left him with Paati. An awkward silence ensued.

With nothing much to do, Aadhi tried to calm his jumpy nerves. He rubbed his palms and slipped into a nervous trance. Soon enough, the sound of half-masticated betel leaf consistently getting smacked against the roof of Paati's mouth kept him company. But too bad for him, it grated on his senses. It was awful and he fought the urge to cover his ears but thankfully, something caught his attention and all else became trivial.

Haasini and her mother walked into the verandah. They were busy engaging in animated chatter. Something big was happening. As if to confirm his prediction, a young man in his late twenties walked out of the very room where the two women had come out from. He carried a big bunch of silk saris and colourful cotton fabric. He took a few steps forward only to rush back into the room to fetch the measuring tape that he had almost forgotten. Just like every other tailor in town, he put it around his neck as if it were a stethoscope on a doctor.

"I feel that simple gold embellishments would look good on your wedding blouse. Would you want me to add them?" he spoke to Haasini while carefully placing the unstitched clothes in his gigantic sling bag.

She looked at her mother who readily approved of the idea with a nod.

"Oh, sure. That does sound good." She was just about to wave him goodbye when her eyes met those of an unexpected guest. Aadhi, however, did not seem very happy. Something was bothering him. He avoided looking at her and chose to greet her mother instead.

"So glad to see you, *kanna*. We received a telegram from your mother two days ago. It was just a general enquiry about our well-being and wedding preparations. She did not seem to mention anything about your visit though," said his soon-to-be mother-in-law. She was happy to see him after almost a month. "It is so good to see you today. And what a coincidence! You chose to arrive at such an auspicious time. *Ravi yogam* began just a few minutes ago."

Aadhi could feel droplets of sweat forming on his temples. The fear of the authority of a mother-in-law was as old as the institution of marriage itself.

"Come along, *maganey*. Take a seat and I'll go prepare fresh dosas." She walked towards the kitchen and asked Haasini to fetch a banana leaf from the storeroom.

"Thank you so much, *Aththai*, but I just had a heavy meal at my friend's place. Some other time, maybe."

"Aah... Amma! Here you are." Raghavan appeared out of nowhere. "Looks like your son-in-law's attempt to surprise you is going really well." His jibe at Aadhi sent ripples of soft laughter across the house. "Let's all get ready to go out, Amma. He is taking us someplace nice."

"Out? A lot of things are pending, Raghu." She addressed him by his nickname. "The wedding is just around the corner. I cannot afford to spend time on outings. You three get going. I'll stay back."

The youngsters stared at each other and then at the mother in disbelief. Did she just ask the three of them to go out with no adult supervision? Not to mention the impending wedding in a month's time.

"Wh-What about Appa? He has not come home yet and we haven't even asked him. Will he approve of this?" Raghavan was still in awe of his mother's response.

"Don't worry about that. I'm sure he will be fine with it, provided you get back home before sunset," his mother assured him.

"Amma, this is not fair! You seem to be giving your darling daughter all the lenience just because she is getting married." Raghavan never cared much about putting a filter on his mouth. But his lighthearted chuckle always managed to balance things out a little bit.

"Well, why not...she is the only daughter I have." She saw him make faces at Haasini who got back at him with equally gravity-defying facial expressions. "Come on, you two. Stop with your antics before I change my mind! Get going and be back on time," she warned.

All it took them was two minutes to stock up a straw bag with a few oranges and a copper water bottle. Aadhi made his way towards the carriage while the siblings were still busy annoying each other. Right before they left, the two of them simultaneously made a dash for the open basket full of fresh red mulberries. Each of them grabbed a handful and hastened towards the dirt road. Outside, the coachman was already in position while Aadhi inspected the reins. Theyn and Nila were beautiful Kathiawari horses. Theyn was almost five but as playful as a two-year-old. Her coat had a soft golden hue, almost as if she had bathed in honey. Her companion Nila, on the other hand, was a three-year-old that had the bearings of a wiser, older horse. She was the colour of the moon; her coat was the shiniest amalgamation of grey, white, and pale blue. Raghavan jumped in and sat right next to the coachman. Aadhi extended his hand as Haasini approached him. She touched his fingers ever so gently and hoped for a smile in return.

But all he said was, "*Paarthu Aerungal.*" He cautioned her to watch her step but not once did he look straight at her.

The following journey was awkward, to say the least. Not a word was spoken between them; quite a contrast to the engaging conversation that Raghavan was having with the coachman. Forty minutes later, they arrived at a green patch of land on the south bank of the river Vaigai.

It was a pleasant morning and the sun graciously greeted the city of Madurai. From the spot where the three of them stood, they could see the south-facing tower of the famous Meenakshi Amman temple. Its historic glory was treasured by young and old alike.

A few other people were present too. A middle-aged man stood in the shallow waters near the bank. He was busy teaching his elder son the art of swimming in flowing waters. Two younger siblings and their mother cheered for the boy as he managed to swim towards his father without much struggle.

"How I wish I was here with my girl too. We could have spent the whole day talking sweet nothings." Raghavan pinched his sister on the elbow.

"Oh, come on. You are too young to even think about girls. Go talk to the horses," Haasini said, twisting his left ear as she pretended to reprimand him.

"Yeah, right! Now that you have found your *Ilavarasan*, you would say this and much more." He pulled her long plaits as she protested and continued, "Well for your information, those horses are great company. If Mama consents, I would like to get back to them."

Aadhi readily agreed and encouraged the young lad to go over to the horses and added, "Would you please get us all some roasted peanuts on your way back?"

"Of course, Mama." Raghavan nodded and walked towards Theyn and Nila.

"Aadhi...what is up with you? Why aren't you talking to me?" Haasini was frustrated and concerned. It was as if he was punishing her for no fault of hers.

Again, silence greeted her.

That was it. She stood up and furiously walked towards the edge of the river. Her shoulders rose and fell as she breathed anger out of her system. As she contemplated on whether to go back to him or to just sit there and wait for that brat of a man to show up, moist lips pressed against her right cheek. The whole of her jumped involuntarily. She turned in a frenzy and her face was only inches away from Aadhi's. He was the only one in the vicinity who had the stomach to do such a thing in full public view. He was so close that she could feel his breath on her lips.

"What if someone sees us?" Her words were a mix of embarrassment and excitement.

"Let them." Aadhi's voice was heavy. He moved in closer. "I am so very sorry for what happened earlier. I just..." he paused and looked away before turning to look at her again. "I just felt jealous. There was this random tailor measuring you up while I sat outside, waiting," he sulked.

She patiently listened as he tried to open up.

"I know it was really immature of me to even think that way but Haasini, I love you more than the world can fathom. The thought of someone else being close to you while I am miles away just turns me into someone I am not." He sighed and shook his head. "Please tell me you have forgiven me." The earnest look in his eyes made her want to plant kisses all over his face.

"I love you, Aadhi. There's no one else I would want to spend every single moment with but you." She smiled and rested her head on his shoulder. "Just cannot wait to get married..."

The excited laughter and the sound of the boys splashing water brought the young lovers back to reality. They settled down and assumed a more agreeable seat.

"Your city is as beautiful as you are my beloved." Aadhi pulled something out of his pocket as he spoke. "It is only fair that I present this to no one else but you."

Haasini gasped when she saw a beautiful maroon pouch that glistened as if it housed a few stray rays of the summer sun. "Oh my God, Aadhi...what is this?"

"Open it." He smiled as he spoke.

Haasini peeped into the pouch and found the prettiest pair of emerald drops.

"Aadhi! These are absolutely beautiful." Her genuine admiration of its craftsmanship was evident in her eyes. "But..." she hesitated before continuing, "These are far too precious."

"And that is precisely why you should have them. Amma wanted to give you these herself but she wasn't able to join me. These are all yours." A second passed before he placed a gentle hand on her cheek and turned her face towards his.

"Happy birthday, *Kannamma*."

"Oh, Aadhi! Thank you...thank you so very much." She hugged him tightly even before she finished her sentence.

Surprised by her open display of affection, he asked her in a hushed voice, "Are you not afraid that people would see us like this?"

"No, I am not and I don't care." She planted a kiss on his left cheek and continued, "We are going to be husband and wife after all."

His shoulder felt moist. He pulled away from the hug and realized that Haasini was crying tears of joy. He was taken aback and did not know what to do.

She prompted him between soft happy sobs, "This is where you hand me your handkerchief."

"Oh right! Of course." He fumbled before pulling out a neat white kerchief that had his initials embroidered on it.

"Thank you," she spoke in the sweetest of childish voices.

"What is that?" Aadhi asked.

"That?"

"Yeah." He motioned towards her nose and laughed heartily. He loved teasing her.

She quickly wiped her nose before playfully pushing him away. "I hate you...you know that, right?"

Aadhi put his hand around her neck and brought her closer. "I love you, too."

The flowing waters gurgled along as the river heard the two of them fill the air with mirth and laughter.

Ketti Melam

10th May, 1915

She was draped in a red Kanchipuram silk sari. The pleats sat comfortably on her lean, feminine frame. Her long wavy locks were plaited into a loose fish braid that was adorned with jasmine flowers tied together to form a luxurious bunch. There was no makeup except for some kohl, face talc, and pomegranate-jelly lipstick. Her skin radiated happiness and that seemed more than sufficient to tell the world that it was her wedding day.

All accessories were kept modest, especially for a Hindu wedding of their time. A gold *nethichuti* with its central piece shaped like a raindrop rested on her forehead. Gold and sapphire earrings complimented her moulded jawline and a chunky gold necklace added an exotic glow to her sleek neck. A gold waist belt accentuated the grandeur of her sari and a set of red and gold bangles completed her look. Thin silver anklets glistened as she held up her sari with red, *maruthani*-painted fingertips. Accompanied by her Amma, cousins, and a big entourage of aunts from near and far, she walked out of her dressing room. Haasini was all set to become Mrs. Aadhisankaran.

At the *Mandapam*, Aadhi was reciting the mantras but his eyes were busy searching for his wife-to-be. There was a time when marrying her felt like a distant dream. His trembling fingers reminded him of the power of destiny. The memory of the first time he saw her was still fresh in his mind. All that followed forged a bond that would unite their hearts for a lifetime. He was so preoccupied with his thoughts that he did not notice her settling down beside him. She gently tapped his elbow, held his sweaty fingers, and looked him straight in the eyes.

Everything will fall into place, have faith—her expression conveyed. He smiled in agreement. The enchanting music of the *thavil* and *nadhaswaram* brought them back to their fairytale bliss. The wedding photographer's 1912 Vest Pocket Kodak caught them blushing.

The Encounter

16th July, 2015

Owing to the fact that all auto-rickshaw drivers think they are the only ones on the road, travelling in such three-wheeled motor vehicles can be stressful. But then, the pain in Akshara's body was making her feel half-dead anyway; standing on a dusty tar road without her phone and wallet did not help either. She took her chances and managed to hail one after several failed attempts.

As the auto drummed its way into town, she asked the driver where they were. But he did not respond. Instead, he kept looking back from the rearview mirror.

Akshara's heart began to pump in terror. "Brother, where are we?" Her voice trembled as she spoke. She asked him again in Tamil, this time a bit louder, "*Anna, enna edam idhu?*" But he remained silent. Panic struck her so hard that fatigue gave way to a shrill cry.

"Stop!"

While he continued to be unresponsive, she pulled him by the collar in an attempt to prevent him from driving any further. But nothing seemed to work.

When all else failed, she decided to jump. Having seen a lot of young men get down from moving buses, she had a fair idea of how to go about it.

"You can do it!" She said out loud and with one swift movement, jumped out just in time to avoid a motorbike. After another bout of disorientation and heavy-headedness, she located the all too familiar archway leading up to *Paati's* place at Kovil Street. Thankfully for her, the yellow wrought-iron gate to her house was not difficult to locate even under such a not-so-optimal circumstance. The gate was already open and she walked in with a sense of urgency.

To her greatest relief, Vinod Mama was right outside the front door. He was busy fastening the laces of his shoes and his face was flushed and puffy.

"Thank God you are here!" Akshara caught her breath and continued, "the car, my wallet, phone, everything is gone." She paused to breathe. Her chest ached with every word she spoke. "I was lying unconscious on the edge of Fort-Road. No one cared to help me."

Unable to stand any longer, she slumped on the stairs on the porch. "We need to lodge a police complaint at the earliest."

As she hoped to catch her breath, she waited for her uncle to respond. Five seconds passed and yet she heard nothing. With great effort, she managed to raise her head to look in his direction. A lone tear found its way to the corner of her nose. She felt betrayed. Not one person was interested in what she had to say. The limit to Akshara's emotional tolerance was breached at that very moment. But she chose to try, one last time and ran up to him with whatever little she had left.

"Mama, wait. Please wait. I need your help." His indifferent expression was a deal breaker. "What on earth is your problem? Talk to me for God's sake," she screamed so loud that it was deafening for her own ears.

Akshara questioned her very existence when Vinod left her behind and sped out of sight on his bike. She dropped to her knees and accepted defeat. Unknown to her though, this was only the tip of the iceberg.

The crisis was beginning to feel very real when someone put a hand on her shoulder. After all the ignoring and walking away, someone was finally there for her. His deep, gentlemanly voice was all too familiar when he said, "Vinod cannot hear you, my child..."

But this cannot be. If he was who she thought he was, she should not be hearing him. Neither should she be feeling his reassuring touch. She knew at once that something dreadful had happened. A heavy cocktail of terror, excitement, relief, and helplessness gripped her. With the greatest fear she had known until then, she turned to her left and saw an old man clad in a white ceremonial *veshti*. The sleeves of his shirt were rolled up and rested around his elbows. His hair and moustache were white as a cotton flower. The calm expression on his face was a stark contrast to the confusion and fear on hers. The wrinkles on his skin were just the way she had last seen them.

Akshara stood in front of a man who looked every bit like *Thatha*...why he was *Thatha*!

The only X factor in this equation was that her grandfather had died a year and three months ago.

She opened her mouth to scream but not one sound escaped.

"Don't be scared, *Kanna*. I am here to help you." He continued to speak in his eerily calm voice. "I do not know a subtler way of saying this...You met with a terrible accident near Fort Road."

Before he could go on any further, Akshara uttered the three words that no human should ever have the misfortune of uttering. "Am I dead?"

"No! Of course not." Thatha walked towards her but stopped midway when he noticed the state she was in. Confusion and fear were smeared all over her face. "Your body is unconscious. Vinod just left to visit you at the hospital," he explained in a gentle tone.

Things were getting real in the most unreal manner. "Is this a dream?"

Thatha smiled his signature lopsided smile, walked up to his granddaughter and held her hands ever so gently. "My child, this is no dream. This is the very place where peace is born, where life beyond the physical nature of your body takes shape. Your family here is so much bigger than you could ever imagine."

He was probably right. No dream could possibly convey the genuine truth in the warmth of his fingers or the depth of his calm voice. "Your soul is free to go wherever it wishes to go. I am here to assist you in every way possible."

Did he just say, soul?

She took a couple of steps backwards as Thatha uttered those words.

"Akshara, my dear, I am not oblivious to the fact that you are scared after all that you have been through. And I am sure you desperately want to go back to being your old self and trust me, that is exactly what I want for you, too. However, for that to happen, you need to let me help you. Let us sit and talk." He looked at her with the kind of love that only grandparents are capable of expressing.

It was all beginning to fall into place. She remembered going out to buy ice cream for her younger cousins. It was a breezy afternoon and there was not much traffic.

Akshara's car whizzed past a few other vehicles when a colourful line of roadside fruit stalls caught her attention. Surprisingly enough, that's all she remembered; at least not until the point when she found herself staring at the sun that hastily descended behind a massive tamarind tree. Her body was stiff from lying flat on the edge of a dirty tar road.

* * *

She looked up at Thatha and noticed that he was still holding her hand as if to tell her that no matter what, he was there to stay. The warmth of his hands reminded her of how much she had missed him.

"Thatha, what happened to me?"

"A water truck went rogue and rammed straight into your car. No one from the living world can see or hear you right now." His voice was calm and deep.

She held on to his right hand as they spoke. The common wall between their house and the adjacent one served as a comfortable hangout place. "Is this what death feels like?" she asked him.

"At least initially, yes."

"What do you mean?" She was worried. Was she dying already?

"You see, post-death experiences are very similar to the various stages of life that an average human is subjected to. One has to go through three different phases before making a transition to the other side." Thatha rubbed his chin as he spoke.

"The other side...What is it like?" Akshara was anxious to hear his response.

"You should not concern yourself with death, my dear. You are not dead. It is a state of limbo that is keeping you here. We will figure out the best way to get you back in form and you will be fit and fine before you know it."

"Are you not afraid, Thatha?"

"Not in the least. Things are simple here. It is life that is complicated."

Akshara forced a smile and tried to nod in agreement. She shifted closer to him and hoped to ask another question when he spoke before she could. "Looks like our folks are back." Thatha was pointing towards his wife.

Rajeswari Paati's face wore a tired, blank expression. As she walked towards the house, Vinod hurried up to her and opened the heavy wrought iron gate.

"You think they are there, at the hospital?" Akshara wanted to know if her parents had flown down from Jaipur.

"Yes. They are here already. Come on now...I cannot let you be bothered by things that are currently not under your control." Thatha tried to veer the topic away from all this mess.

Her sombre expression did not change till he said, "I am taking you to my ancestral village tomorrow. There's someone I want you to meet." He winked and got off the wall on which they had been sitting all the while.

"Who is it?"

"Let us just say we are going to keep that as a surprise."

"Why can't we go right now? Are we not supposed to be spirits who can go wherever we want, whenever we want?"

Thatha laughed as if she had just cracked the funniest joke ever. He took his own sweet time with his laughter riot before turning towards Akshara with an earnest smile.

"Kanna, being in the spirit world does not give you special powers. Well, sure, you do feel a lot more energetic and much more positive about all that the universe has to offer. But that does not give you a free ticket to Stan Lee's world of superheroes. You are as much a spirit now as you were human before. If you were not a bird in the living world, then there's no way you are going to be able to fly in the spirit world."

The Ghost in White

17th July, 2015

"Are you ready?"

"Yes, sir. Got nothing to pack anyway. Feels good to travel so light." Akshara was feeling much better than the night before. She moved and spoke faster, with greater energy. "Are we going to walk all the way to your village?"

"No, we are taking the bus." He was already six paces ahead of her.

"Sounds good." She followed him as he took light, unhurried steps.

"So, Thatha, how often do you visit your place?"

"I visit pretty much every time our ancestors hold a conclave. It is to welcome those who are ready to start the second leg of their post-death journey. I must say, it is a big event."

"Wow...Okay."

"Akshara, I see a bus. Let us pace up."

She walked faster and asked him hesitantly, "You are not the one leaving...are you?"

"Of course not. The conclave is not for me but for someone very special."

She let out a sigh of relief. But a moment later, curiosity crept in. "Who is it for?"

"Surprises ought to remain surprises." He winked and challenged her to run towards the bus stop. The man was running too fast for someone his age.

"Mr. Old Man, wait for me!" She was not sure if all this was her second chance at life or at death. But either way, it was liberating to run alongside her grandfather.

"But the bus is full," Akshara noted as they reached the bus stop.

"I guess so," Thatha replied. Mischief, however, was brewing in his greyish-blue eyes. "Not that anyone would know even if we sat on them or the driver's seat but I have something else in mind. Let's have some harmless fun today. To think that this would be objectionable in the world of the living makes it all the more interesting."

Akshara held her breath as she saw him climb up to the roof of the bus.

"Come along already." He held out his right hand and encouraged her to loosen up for once.

She took a few steps forward and then backtracked. "I can't do this. This is too risky. I can't…" Before she could finish, the bus started moving. Panic struck her like a bolt of lightning. She froze and had no clue what to do next.

"Grab the window rails!" Thatha acted swiftly and prepared to pull her up. "You can do this, my girl." He was loud and clear.

His voice helped Akshara snap out of her inertia. She managed to run to the nearest window and gripped the rails with all her strength. Thatha stood right on top and pulled her up without much struggle.

"This…" Akshara paused to catch her breath. "This is THE most adventurous thing I have ever done." She let out a sigh of relief and laughed aloud. The excitement was hard to contain. "Thatha, I am loving this already!"

"Wait till we reach the village. It's going to be so much more spectacular."

* * *

"Why Thatha, this place is such a beauty! Why didn't you bring me out here much earlier?"

"Even I wonder why I never did that." He shrugged and continued, "But I'm glad you are here today."

She was awestruck. The village was beautiful, to say the least. All *veedhis* were clean and well kept. Women were busy drawing *kolams* in front of their homes while children rubbed their sleepy eyes and tagged along with their mothers. A bunch of young men were already busy playing cricket on the other end of the street. As they walked through a large canopy of mango trees, Thatha turned into a patron of the dramatic arts and with much fanfare, gestured towards the road ahead. Welcome to *Valimaioor*, a signpost said, "The land of the strong."

* * *

They walked for a good two kilometres before he paused and spoke in a calm voice, "This is the place. I am sure she's in here."

"Who, Thatha?"

"You'll see in a while. Wait here. She will be really happy to meet you." Thatha was so much more excited than Akshara was. With a few quick paces, he disappeared into the vastness of a rock-cut structure ahead. It was close to three stories high and had intricately carved panels all over it. The mammoth monument was surrounded by a well-kept garden. On the far end of the green patch, an old lady was busy tending to the soil. Her back was slightly hunched and her grey cotton sari was loosely draped. Her face, however, shone as bright as the sun on a pleasant summer morning.

The woman's fingers moved like scissors while plucking a handful of quack grass out of the freshly watered soil. Akshara walked up to her and sat close by. Sitting there and waiting it out till Thatha arrived was the only thing left to be done.

The older woman scanned every patch of grass around her and got up to leave only after conducting another round of inspection .Akshara's eyes followed her fragile frame as she walked back towards the stone structure. Just as the old woman reached the entrance that was guarded by two heavy wooden doors, a young couple walked in her direction. They smiled and bent down to touch her feet.

"*Enna Raja*, how are you both?" the elderly woman was all smiles.

"All good, Paati. Anita has secured a job in Delhi. We plan to move there by the end of this week." The man gestured towards the woman next to him.

Akshara could not help but notice how good they looked in traditional Tamil attire. The young woman was dressed in a blue silk sari with broad golden borders. The man looked sharp in his white *veshti* and brown shirt. Each of them held a piece of coconut and some flowers. Streaks of fresh *kumkumam* were visible on their foreheads....

"What is this place?" Akshara thought out loud as she had gotten used to speaking in the absence of an active listener. The place had caught her by surprise and she was looking around with great anticipation. While trying to put the pieces together, she also noticed a stepwell to her right. On the other side of the garden, a big herd of cows were grazing.

"This has to be a temple," she spoke to herself again. The realization was so overwhelming that she got up to her feet. The sanctum was too beautiful for admiration from afar. The simple act of walking, however, was beginning to prove dangerous. Akshara felt as if someone had tied her lungs in a knot. Her eyes failed her when she saw a bunch of people in pink scrubs walking in and around the temple. A series of beds magically popped out of nowhere. Multiple devices stood around those beds and every once in a while, a persistent beep brought those machines to life. Her legs gave away when she found herself standing on someone's chest. The person's body was covered in loose green attire. The legs were swollen red with what looked like multiple screws jutting out every few inches. A long tube ran from under the drape and met a transparent bag that was half-filled with murky, yellowish-red fluid. The hands too were not spared the agony of tubes, needles, and screws.

A woman in pink scrubs ran up to the duty doctor and announced, "Her MAP is dipping. We need to pace her up."

As they rushed towards her, the horror of being on someone's chest caught up with Akshara. She fought her rising fears and stumbled while trying to get off the person. Her hands and legs froze when she accidentally looked at the unconscious, almost lifeless body below her. It was Akshara herself.

Her left eye was swollen red with traces of blood around it. Big bruises were plastered all over her face. Everything was scary but the sight of what the doctors did to her body was even scarier. They injected something into the central line while frantically working with the ventilator. "We need to get her ready for a scan. I suspect greater cardiogenic complications," the doctor in green scrubs announced with a sense of urgency. He continued to instruct a few more things but Akshara was losing her balance already. She tried to stay rooted to the spot, unable to think until finally, Thatha hastened towards her. A woman ran by his side too. It was still too hazy for Akshara to see her face clearly but she heard her voice distinctly.

"Akshara, it's okay. We are right here." She spoke while lightly squeezing the pseudo flesh on her pseudo shoulders. "Look in my direction, *Kannama*. Look at me. Focus and you will be back with us."

Akshara juggled between razor-sharp squinting and staring till her eyeballs almost fell out of the socket. She gasped as she noticed the young woman's face. Her skin shimmered as if it were covered with gold dust. She was dressed in a dusty pink saree with intricate lace detailing.

"How do you feel now? I hope you are here with us entirely." The sound of her voice calmed Akshara's jumpy nerves.

No beds, no scrubs or screws and stitches. The temple stood ahead without any nurses and duty doctors around. With considerable effort, Akshara replied in as audible a voice as possible, "Yeah…I am back."

Thatha patiently stood by the two women and waited for his granddaughter to feel better.

Akshara opened her mouth to speak again when the other woman gave her a tight hug. "It is so…so good to finally meet you, *Kanna*. Sorry that you had to see yourself like that. But don't you worry…okay? We are going to set this right."

She paused for a moment and kissed Akshara on the forehead. "I am Haasini, your great-grandmother."

"Meet my mother," Thatha said, backing her. He was smiling ear to ear. "And she is right. You are going to be absolutely fine. Don't let the sight of that ICU discourage you."

Haasini looked younger than Akshara and there she was, introducing herself as the great-grandmother.

"Not even in my wildest dream would I have imagined a reunion like this!" Akshara exclaimed.

"Neither would I," she said as she caressed Akshara's forehead.

"Come, let's get you inside. Mother is eager to speak to you about a few things before she leaves." Thatha was a lot calmer than he was a few minutes ago.

"Grand...great mother...I mean great grandmother..." Akshara fumbled and was at a loss for words.

"Oh dear, call me Haasini. That will do." Haasini laughed with lightness. She held Akshara's hand and helped her get back up.

"Umm...Haasini, are you the one passing over to the other side today?" Akshara felt a constant throbbing in her forehead as she spoke.

"After we are done talking, I certainly am." Haasini was all smiles.

As the trio walked towards the sanctum, Akshara noticed the old lady from the garden. Another woman was seated facing her. They were busy handling a bulky wooden pestle, fashioned like a long, stout club. A fresh batch of unpolished rice was being ground into a paste. With every thump, one of the women passed the pestle over to the other, while pushing the coarse paste back to the centre with the other free hand. What caught Akshara's attention was the mortar. It was a rock that sprawled over an area big enough to accommodate a modest, single-room house. A neat hollow in the middle of it served as the grinding space. Closer observation revealed that the two women were actually sitting on the flat section of the mortar.

"Who are they? I saw the old woman earlier. She was tending to the garden and then a young couple spoke to her with much reverence." Akshara turned to Haasini with her question.

"She's Selvi, the temple caretaker, one of the oldest elders of the village. She is respected by one and all. She's preparing my favourite *prasadam*," Thatha quipped even before Haasini could speak.

"Ahem, your grandpa used to be crazy about her back in the days," Haasini made no effort to suppress her smile.

"Oh come on, Amma..." Thatha was visibly blushing. "I was not crazy about her and all that. We were just good friends."

The last line was quite a giveaway and Akshara asked the next obvious question. "If you two were such good friends, how did you meet grandma?"

"Aah! That's a crazy story in itself. It was a chance encounter. She was just nineteen but her generosity and intellect were far beyond her years."

Haasini and Akshara held on to his hand on either side and walked towards the central courtyard; for they knew that whether a man is dead or alive, he would always fall short of words while describing the depth of his love for the love of his life.

Going Back

"I'll leave you two ladies to catch up. In the meantime, I shall go meet Kandasamy. He passed away this morning." Thatha spoke earnestly.

"Don't you worry, Siddhama. Your granddaughter will be safe with me," Haasini teased him.

"Alright then. Have fun." He gave Akshara a tight hug and set off to meet his newly deceased friend.

Haasini tapped Akshara's hand and enquired, "I hope you're feeling okay?"

She hesitated before admitting her lack of adult conversational skills. "I am really awful at sustaining conversations even in the physical world. I am supposed to be dead, almost. Not really sure how to feel right now..."

"In that case, I hope you won't mind me leading the conversation." Haasini's childish enthusiasm was too sweet to ignore. "And you will be fine and healthy before you know it. Don't you talk about death again." She smiled reassuringly.

Akshara nodded in agreement. "I would love to know everything about you…" She wanted to know as to why her great-grandmother was holding on to her bodily form for close to a century.

"Maybe you should slow down your train of thoughts." She winked and extended her right hand towards Akshara. "Let's take a walk…shall we?"

They held hands and walked on the paved outer verandah of the temple complex. A steady stream of devotees was making its way to the shrine and after every few steps, Akshara paused to make way for them. It was quite unnecessary but she was the least interested in letting someone go through her invisible body.

"Well, to answer your question, I have been around for ninety-eight years because I had to meet you." Her face lit up as she spoke further, "When my husband died and we were reunited after decades, I thought that maybe that was it. But it was not long before he crossed over and I was left behind. Last year when your grandfather and I were reunited, I thought that maybe that was finally it—that having met my son, I was ready to leave. But then again, nothing happened."

"How did I help you decide the right time for your departure?" Akshara looked at her the way a little child would look at her parent while asking the most fascinating questions.

"Yesterday, a group of messenger souls informed me about your arrival. I did not really know how to react at first. A few moments passed when I noticed that my left palm was beginning to evaporate. That is when I asked them to inform your grandfather. He knew that I did not have much time and arranged for this meeting at the earliest." She wore a neutral expression as she spoke.

She raised the fabric of her sari and revealed a partially missing hand. Whatever remained was disintegrating like gold dust being blown by a steady gush of wind. Surprisingly, the shimmery yellow particles were blowing upwards.

"That looks scary!" Akshara was alarmed as she examined Haasini's fast-disappearing limb.

"It is not all that bad, you know...just a slight bit tingly."

As soon as the initial shock subsided, Akshara jumped to the next question. "These messengers you just spoke about...who are they?"

"They are our ancestors. In the absence of a physical form, they move around swiftly, unrestricted. You will get to meet them during the congregation."

Akshara was unsure of how she must acknowledge this new piece of information. "Have you been here ever since you died?" Her heart ached when she realised that Haasini had existed in this state of limbo for almost a century.

"That would be correct." The older woman responded in her sing-song voice. Akshara observed the woman in front of her and earnestly tried to understand the paranormal aura of her great-grandmother. Her jet-black irises were turning golden and dusty. As the first rays of the morning sun fell, Haasini's skin had become translucent. It was like she was made of honey and gold dust. "I cannot help but think that I am probably one of the lucky few who get to meet their ninety-eight-year-old grandfather and twenty-something great-grandmother."

"Twenty-three, actually." A riot of laughter followed. It was so in sync that it made them laugh even harder.

This is War

20th April, 1916

The earth pressed down on him, filled his nose and mouth and enveloped him in darkness. Perhaps it was a blessing. It meant the horrors were over. He could let go of life and embrace oblivion. How he yearned to expel the fear that had invaded his body and mind these past months. An all-pervading fear to be fought every second of every day. His men must never see this weakness. They depended on him to lead, to keep them alive in the hell of trench warfare on the Western Front. It was his duty to fight, to fight for India, to fight for the sepoys under his command. For Haasini.

Aadhi jerked his head up against the earth, felt it give slightly away, and managed to spit the soil out of his mouth. *Haasini.* The thought of her was like being struck by lightning. He could not, would not die in a filthy dugout in France. He could not leave his great love all alone in the world. Aadhi started to struggle against the weight of earth all about him but it was impossible to escape its embrace. He could feel the panic rising, taking a grip over his body and there was only little he could do to stop it. He was going to die a terrible death, Aadhi was sure of that.

Haasini, Ponnu, forgive me.

Suddenly Aadhi was seized by his left boot. He felt a tight grip on both legs and then he was being dragged backwards. He was rolled onto his back and water splashed on his face to wash away the dirt. Aadhi gasped. Fresh air tinged with cordite rushed into his lungs. He opened his eyes to see the grinning face of *Havildar* Pallavan Devar looking down at him.

"Thank *Lakshmi* you're alive." Aadhi felt a sudden warmth towards the Havildar. His mud-splattered uniform, bushy grey moustache, and fierce eyes were comforting at that moment. Devar had been in the Indian Cavalry for over 20 years and Aadhi had come to rely on his soldiering experience. He could smell the Germans a mile away. "They are on the way. Come on, sir."

Aadhi got unsteadily to his feet and the familiar sounds of battle crowded his senses once more. The thump of shells exploding in the mud, the non-stop rat-tat-tat of machinegun fire. Now it came back to him. He had been in the command dugout when the first German shells screamed down, exploding, and pulverizing the trench network. One must have landed close to the command dugout, the shockwave burying him alive, and knocking him unconscious. Aadhi snapped open the battered leather holster at his side and pulled out his Webley service revolver. The weight of the weapon felt good and reassuring. He spun the chamber to make sure it was free of dirt and then set off after the *Havildar* who was just disappearing around a corner of the trench.

The whiz and buzz of bullets passing just overhead were hard to ignore. It was a clear indication that the German infantry was out of their trenches and attacking across no man's land. The very thought of no man's land made Aadhi shiver. The waste ground of bomb craters, rotting corpses and limbs, barbed wire, and broken and abandoned equipment separated the two warring armies. The stench of death lay heavy in the air but Aadhi was so used to it he didn't even notice.

He soon caught up with *Havildar* Devar who was busy pulling the other fallen sepoys to their feet. They had to meet the Germans head-on with bullets and bayonets. Aadhi moved onto the firing step and peered through a tiny slit in the sandbag wall, which formed the trench's forward defences and protected the soldiers from shrapnel and snipers. To his left, the men were shooting into the smoke. The fusillade of fire from the sepoys' Lee Enfield rifles sounded a bit like machinegun fire. Fifteen rounds a minute and every man in the company was well-trained and adept at scoring a kill at over 600 yards. At this point, only 400 yards separated Aadhi's men in the line from the Germans' trenches.

The smoke from the shelling was starting to clear and dim figures started to emerge. It was an eerie sight, like ghosts appearing and disappearing, in and out of the fog of war. Bullets raked the top of the sandbags. These were battle-hardened soldiers clad in grey greatcoats, wearing spiked helmets, and carrying Mauser rifles with the terrible Butcher Blade Bayonet attached. The Imperial German Army was adept at slaughter and the Fatherland's *Gefreiters*, the ordinary privates, were highly motivated and determined. They were brave men but then so were the men of the Indian Army.

"Here they come!" yelled *Havildar* Devar, who was nestled behind the heavy Vickers machine gun. He started to fire burst after burst, the muzzle spitting bullets into the smoke.

To Aadhi's left, he could see the sepoys Kumaran and Velu firing steadily, working the bolt action of their rifles to send fresh rounds into the breach. They appeared calm despite the wild glances they sent Aadhi's way. On the right, Lance-Naik Pillai started tossing grenades over the lip of the parapet. Pillai was a giant of a man with the heart and courage of a Bengal Tiger. He loved battle and was born for the fight.

The company strength was only 75 men, a mix of sepoys and cavalry *sowars* thrown together to plug a 300-yard gap in the British lines. This was the second week of the German offensive and whole battalions of Indian and British soldiers had died holding these positions. Makeshift platoons were formed into companies and every man able to carry and fire a rifle was pressed into service, wounded or not. A couple of English soldiers were scattered somewhere along the trench. Boys really, not more than 18, but right now Aadhi needed every gun he could muster.

The noise was deafening. The German artillery lifted its barrage towards the rear echelons in an effort to stop any reinforcements from reaching the front lines. Flashes of gunfire reached out of the smoke and the first German burst into sight in front of the trench. Calmly, Aadhi aimed his revolver and fired. The .45 bullet struck the man in the chest and burst out his back in a mist of blood. He fell into a crumpled heap.

More and more of the enemy now emerged from the smoke, screaming and firing, running towards them. Aadhi emptied his revolver, reloaded it, and emptied it again. The Vickers and *Havildar* Devar were all that was keeping back the attacking hoard. Bodies started to pile up in front of the trench as Devar walked the machine gun back and forth. It was slaughter and Aadhi grinned as the fury of battle overtook him.

A German stick grenade landed in the trench and the consequent explosion was appalling. The concussion hurled Aadhi off the fire step and sent him crashing into the rear wall of the trench. Winded, he gasped for air and staggered back to his feet. Velu had taken the brunt of the detonation and his bloody broken body lay still and unmoving. Aadhi hadn't known the man long but he had been a comrade in arms and now he was a twisted wreck of blood, bone, and guts smeared in the dirt. Aadhi felt numb. He looked towards the charging enemy. They seemed to be moving in slow motion. A rage gripped him.

"Let's kill the bastards!" screamed Aadhi, grabbing a short spade from the fire step and rolling over the top of the sandbags. Devar and the giant Pillai followed, their blood lusting in full cry. The three Indians crashed into the enemy who was advancing singly and in small groups now, having been thinned out by the defenders' fire. Pillai thrust his bayonet right through one German's body then raising a boot, kicked the corpse off the blade. He rushed off into the smoke.

Aadhi found himself among a group of attackers. He swung his spade wildly and the side sliced into a neck. Blood splattered onto Aadhi's face but he didn't notice. He swung his spade again and this time his target's head came clean off and the body stood stiff as blood fountained out of it. He spun to his right and cleaved a face open. The man fell screaming to the ground, his spiked helmet rolling away. Aadhi felt nothing at all. He coldly hacked down on the wounded man's neck and the screaming stopped.

The rest of the Company climbed out of the protection of the trenches and with a rifle, bayonet, and trench knife fell upon the Germans. No quarter was asked and none was given in the hand-to-hand fighting that followed. Smoke swirled, screams of the wounded and dying and the crack of rifle fire filled the air. "For India, for freedom," screamed Devar. Then, the Havildar was dead. His chest was torn open by point-blank gunfire; his body flung into the mud like a ragdoll. Aadhi witnessed the death of the man who had saved his life in the dugout. He roared like a wounded tiger. Gripped by anguish, rage, and the need for vengeance, Aadhi lost what little control remained in him and charged forward shouting with wild abandon. Germans turned and scattered. The apparition before them wasn't human. It was a beast from the depths of hell butchering men left and right.

Seeing the small company of Indians heroically fighting their way across no man's land, the rest of the British line rose out of the trenches. At first, it was one or two here and there, then it turned into a flood. The entire British line stretching for half a mile streamed over the top and crashed into the enemy. The Germans reeled from the unexpected mass counterattack sparked by the small group of Indian Army volunteers. Their troops faltered, stopped, and then the *Tommies* were among them, killing, screaming, and dying. It could have been a medieval battle. Thousands of men were gripped in mortal face-to-face fighting, hacking, slashing, and stabbing; blood and guts spilt amid the mud and craters of a small strip of French soil.

Aadhi was splattered head to toe in blood, bits of flesh, and entrails. He stopped to catch his breath and looked wildly about him. Everywhere men were locked in combat. There was no mercy to be found here today.

Aadhi was suddenly lifted into the air and hurled through the smoke by some unseen force. He crashed to the ground and rolled into a crater. Darkness rushed in.

* * *

Aadhi came back to a world of silence. The fighting seemed to have stopped. He had no idea how long he had been unconscious. But he was alive, *thank Lakshmi*, thought Aadhi. He sat up and looked about. Much to his surprise, he saw Pillai squatting at the bottom of the crater, his hand outstretched clutching a canteen. Aadhi gulped the cooling water, nodding his appreciation. He didn't trust his ability to speak but was forestalled from saying anything by another voice.

"Ah, awake are you now, laddie." It wasn't a question and the Scottish brogue was unmistakable. "One hell of a scrap, eh? But we're alive although for how long is not for anyone's guess."

A shell exploded nearby, sending mud and bits of bodies raining down. Aadhi slipped to the bottom of the deep bomb crater to join Pillai and the Scotsman.

"Thought you were dead, sir," said the giant Indian. "Not sure how many men made it. The Germans opened us up with everything but we stopped their assault cold, sir."

"Aye, now we are trapped in no man's land at the bottom of a bloody bomb crater." The Scotsman was squat and broad-shouldered and covered in the filth of battle. "Saw you boys giving it to them and just had to join the fight. Highlanders like the fight. I'm Adair Mackay, Captain Ninth Battalion of the Highland Light Infantry. They call us the Dandy Ninth."

"Well, Mackay, you don't look so dandy right now." Aadhi nodded in the direction of the *Lance-Naik*. "That's Corporal Pillai and I'm Captain Aadhisankaran Chettiyar on special detachment from the Indian Army."

"Pleased to meet you both and you're no picture either." Mackay laughed in a gruff but friendly manner. "Special detachment, you say? Aye, we could do with more like you, that's for sure. Thing is, we are in a bit of a pickle, see?"

Just then the chatter of machinegun fire rang out, breaking the silence that hung over the battlefield. *A bit of a pickle is an understatement*, thought Aadhi. They were in the middle of no man's land, hunkered down in a crater with trenches just a hundred yards away packed with Germans all wanting payback for their failed attack and the loss of their comrades. Gone were the days when medics could collect the wounded. Sticking your head up then would have guaranteed a sniper putting a bullet in it.

"It will be dark soon." Aadhi pointed out. "That will be our best chance to make it back to our lines. If we try to move out now, we're dead men."He wanted to say something more but could not speak another word. Something was wrong with him, Aadhi could feel it in his body. He started shaking. He couldn't control the shaking. It got worse and a feeling of utter *dread* took hold. He wanted to get up and run. Paranoid anxiety gripped him at that moment.

"Grab him, Corporal." Mackay snapped at Pillai. "Hold him tight. It's the shell shock."

The giant arms that enveloped Aadhi were like steel bands. They held him fast, strong but at the same time gentle. "I got you, sir, I got you."

Aadhi was somewhat surprised at the softness of the Corporal's voice. It was somehow reassuring but at the same time, humiliating. *Shell shock.* He had heard the term before, usually by army doctors, just before the firing squad dispatched those branded cowards. *That's not me*, Aadhi shivered. *I'm no coward.*

"Hahaha!" Mackay grinned at Aadhi. "Nothing to worry about, laddie. I've had the shakes more times than I care to imagine. I know what you're thinking. Coward. Well, you're not. But if the shakes are all you get then be grateful. There are the night terrors so bad you wouldn't want to sleep."

"Damn your eyes, Mackay." Aadhi managed to grin back at the Highlander as his shaking started to subside. He was back in control, exhausted but in control. Pillai released him from the bearhug and slid back. "Thank you, Corporal. I owe you."

"Think nothing of it, sir, I've seen this many times during the frontier wars." Pillai looked at him squarely in the eyes in a matter-of-fact way. "It's the price we pay. Believe me or not but I have had the shock and shakes twice since we arrived here."

"You?" Aadhi looked at the giant in total disbelief. "I find that too hard to believe."

"Believe it, sir." At that moment, Aadhi caught a glimpse of the man behind the soldier's mask and he felt moved by what he saw. There was pain in those eyes, a weariness of life maybe. But the army was all Pillai knew and all he would ever know. The realisation the Corporal would probably die here in France was like a punch in the belly.

"Would you like to consider working on my estate when all of this is over?" Aadhi meant what he said. He took a deep breath before continuing, "You have seen far too much blood and gore, Pillai. You deserve better."

Before the *Lance-Naik* could reply, there was a loud crack of a Mauser above them. Aadhi spun around, his hand going for his revolver. It wasn't there. He'd lost it in the melee of battle. Standing on the lip of the crater above them was a lone figure. The spiked helmet was unmistakable. There was a whir of movement from Mackay and the attacker clutched at his neck, sank to his knees, and rolled into the crater. The Highlander reached across and pulled a knife from the German's neck.

"Bastard, Jerry." Mackay spat, turned to Aadhi and froze. "Ah, no, no…"

Pillai lay on his back staring sightlessly skyward. A small hole in his forehead told its own story. Aadhi felt a single unbidden tear trickle down his left cheek. He was a man changed forever by this war. He had witnessed men's inhumanity. His experience of the base animal instincts of survival and cruelty. The horror of death, the killing he had taken part in—his hands would be forever bloody. The pain in his chest was like a lance being thrust into his very soul.

"It's dark now, laddie, and we need to go." Mackay put a gentle hand on his shoulder but Aadhi shrugged it off and cradled Pillai's bloody head on his lap. "If we don't go now Captain Chettiyar, we'll be joining our dead friend here."

Harsh words but they snapped Aadhi out of his trance. The Highlander was right. He had no right to make Haasini a widow. He had to survive this war, this carnage. He got to his feet. Then a chilling and real thought struck home. *What if he survived the fighting just to lose his mind, his very soul?*

"Let's go, Mackay."

The Highlander nodded and dropped to his belly, motioning Aadhi to do the same. If they were to get back to the British lines alive, they would have to crawl all the way through the mud, the dead, the gore of battle, and pray a sentry didn't shoot them by mistake when they got there.

"That's more like it, laddie. I'll stand you a bottle of scotch when we get back." Mackay grinned at him and then rolled over the lip of the crater and disappeared from the site. Aadhi smiled to himself. He didn't drink alcohol but could appreciate the sentiment behind the Highlander's offer. It was time to move. Aadhi steeled himself and silently followed Mackay into the night...

Old Blaze

18th February, 1919

It was unlike any other day for Haasini. She was busy resetting the pleats of her blue sari. Aadhi would be home any moment and she had to look her immaculate best. But neither the cheery blue of her attire nor the ruby red of her lips managed to lift her mood. Even after eight attempts, the pleats just did not sit right. She slumped on the cot behind her, still holding a part of the untied fabric.

"He's here! I saw him from the garden. He just crossed the park and will be home any moment!" shouted an excited Ambica who came running upstairs. She was in for a surprise when she saw Haasini's face buried in her palms.

"Amma, is everything okay?" asked a concerned Ambica.

Haasini was trembling. Her shiny, silvery wet cheeks indicated that she had been crying for quite some time. Ambica was more of a companion than her house help at the villa. Nakshatra Illam was one of the most attractive houses on Saalai Street. Its walls bore fading traces of maroon that complemented the bold white and pink bougainvillaea that adorned the fences. "What is it, Amma?" Ambica asked again, this time with even greater concern.

After a moment's hesitation, Haasini spoke in a soft weepy voice. "My husband is back from war. I have been yearning to see him, dreaming about this moment every single day for the last two years but now...I'm afraid! Not one letter of mine could reach him in the last ten months. And not once was he allowed to take a leave from all the blood and gore. I heard about him only through those numerous visits to the Madras Headquarters. How will he react? What am I supposed to say to him?"

She bit her lip and stared at the black and white wedding photograph on her dressing table. "What if...what if he doesn't love me anymore?"

"Please don't let all these thoughts bother you. Everything is going to be fine. Let me help you get ready before Ayya gets home." Ambica spoke with a cheery smile.

The sari was finally under control and the tears too were successfully tamed to a great extent. A few wild streaks did manage to break out every now and then. Confident that she would not cry anymore, Haasini picked up her vanity case. After a couple of seconds of foraging, she pulled out a small glass jar filled with vermillion paste. She swished her right ring finger on its soft, cake-like surface a couple of times and then guided it to her forehead. With utmost precision, she drew a perfectly sized red solid circle between her eyebrows. The mirror reflected her flawless complexion.

"Ayya will be happy to see you after so long...I am sure he must have missed the sight of your lovely face!"

Before she could continue with more praises, the heavy mahogany door to the mansion was pushed open. Haasini shot one look at Ambica and walked towards the stairs. Aadhi was back at last.

She descended the last flight of stairs and saw a man dressed in khaki pants, a plain white shirt, and a pair of tattered ankle boots. A faded canvas backpack rested against his legs. His right hand had a swollen, reddish-brown scar that ran from the tip of his thumb all the way to the elbow. Across the length of the scar, large red marks at regular intervals indicated that the cut was deep and had required to be stitched up. One look at his arm and anyone could tell that the wound was crudely sutured as if it were a jute bag that must be sealed before its contents could spill over.

Haasini had not anticipated his war-torn appearance. The remnants of the gruesome reality of the war continued to suck the life out of her husband as if they were leeches. She ran towards him and hugged his battered body. The separation had been painful and now that he was back, the strength of her emotions shook her as if she were having a convulsion.

Aadhi hesitated for a moment before placing his hand on her shoulder. "It's okay. I am back now." He patted the nape of her neck a couple of times before continuing, "I am fine...stop crying." The response was curt with a hint of frustration. It was far from the ideal emotional reunion she had imagined. She was taken aback by his disconnected reaction. It was disappointing but she knew that this was not reason enough to lose heart. He was just back home and all he needed was lots of love and good food...at least that's what she thought.

She bent down to pick up his bag, stood back up, and held his hand in hers. "My dear, I am glad you are home." She forced a smile and continued, "Let's go eat. You must be hungry."

Aadhi followed her into the kitchen without uttering a word. There was none left to be spoken.

* * *

Hyena in the Dark

24th December, 1919

The soldiers were huddled behind a thick slab of wood that served as their dinner table. A pack of spotted hyenas stood on the other side. In the blink of an eye, the hyenas attacked the men and bore their strong jaws into human flesh, bringing them to the ground one by one. Aadhi was on the extreme left, watching them twitch and bleed while they were being mercilessly devoured. It was a misfortune that they were all alive when their bodies were being torn apart. Unlike the big cats, the hyena is not known to follow the laws of hunting.

When the screams finally died off along with the ebbing breaths of his comrades, Aadhi was the last one standing. He stood there motionless when one of the hyenas took deliberate, menacing steps towards him. He prepared himself for a nasty fight. Better to die fighting than to die in fear, he thought. As if to validate this, the animal focused its black beady eyes on him for a good five seconds before pouncing. He woke up before its teeth could fully sink into his shoulder. His eyes scanned the bedroom, just to make sure that no ghastly creatures were around him.

He sat on his bed while his feet touched the floor. Right in the middle of a debate on whether to slouch back and risk another nightmare or to go over to the estate earlier than usual, he felt Haasini's fingers running over his back. A couple of years ago under the same circumstances, he would have hugged her tight and settled back in bed. But none of that was to happen that morning.

"Aadhi, is everything alright?" she asked. She was a bit more concerned than usual.

"Yes...couldn't sleep, that's all," he replied. His indifferent tone worried her even more.

There was a long silence. Haasini knew all too well that it was high time for them to start having frank conversations. He must open up for her to be able to help.

She got up and went over to the other side of the bed. Her nightgown was oversized but that did not stop her baby bump from making its presence felt. After a brief struggle, she managed to pull out a footrest that stood in front of the dressing table and placed it in front of him. Her heavily pregnant belly tugged at the fabric of her nightgown but she somehow managed to seat herself on the footrest.

Aadhi was visibly uncomfortable with all that she was up to. "You should not be doing that. It would be better if you got back in bed...you need to rest." He got up and extended his hands hoping to lift her up but she resisted.

She looked straight into his eyes and said, "We need to talk."

"We can talk all you want but for now, I would like to help you get back to bed."

His reaction was quite unexpected. In the eight months of her pregnancy, he rarely involved himself in her well-being. He was so lost in his own deliberate inaction that he never concerned himself with anything even remotely related to her. There were times when she wanted to ask him upfront as to why he got her pregnant in the first place but then realised that it was a blessing in disguise. If it wasn't for the awkward events of that one drunken night, she would still have been crying herself to sleep for not being able to have a child. Plus, confronting him would only push him deeper into the abyss of a disconnected existence. This frustratingly real piece of logic kept Haasini's emotions in check every time Aadhi's indifference caused her pain.

This particular night, however, he did not just talk her out of sitting down on the footrest but also showered his concern over how she should not be stressing herself too much. He was a lot more interactive than usual. Very carefully, he helped her maintain balance while she got up and escorted her to the other side of the bed. Once he was sure she was comfortably settled, he reached out to the nightstand and plucked a copper water bottle.

He handed it to her and spoke in a gentle voice, "There you go...drink it up."

Haasini took a few gulps and handed the bottle back to him. She was more afraid than surprised at his sudden change of behaviour. The more she thought about it, the more it bothered her to an extent that she could not fight back her tears anymore. "Aadhi..." she paused a moment before continuing, "I cannot understand you these days. One moment you behave as if you loathe me and the very next, you do all this for me. I am scared..."

Aadhi was silent for a long while. It was Haasini's unwavering teary-eyed stare that coaxed him into talking. "I really don't know. I just don't feel like myself anymore." He stammered. His eyes wore a blank expression once again.

"I know how tough the last few years have been for you..." she squeezed his right hand gently and continued, "But you're home now, Aadhi, and I am here for you. Please... open up to me." Haasini got up to hug him but was turned down by a beast that knew no other emotion but rage. He pushed her to the wall and let out a loud shriek. His eyes had turned crimson with rage.

"You know nothing!" His voice bore no resemblance to the man she knew. "You cannot understand how it feels to shoot another human and see him choke on his own blood. It's impossible for you to comprehend the pain of seeing your comrades die or worse, carry their severed limbs back to the camp, hoping that the medic could do the impossible. Don't you dare say you know, damn it!"

He punched the wall right behind Haasini and little crumbs of plaster fell on her shoulders. Depressions appeared on the wall as Aadhi's injured knuckles bled.

She looked at this creature that stood in front of her.

What has he become?

Her initial impulse was to run out of the room to wake up Ambica who stayed on the other side of the road. The shock, however, was far too paralysing. After what seemed like an eternity, she caught her breath. Holding on to her pregnant belly, she bolted towards the door.

He was nothing like the man she once loved. Tears blurred her sight so much that she lost her footing on the stairs and narrowly missed a painful fall. Too much was at stake and her priority was to protect her unborn child from this beast of a man. She was fully prepared to send a telegram to her parents' house the next morning. There was no way she could stay with him any longer. Her mother had insisted on more than one occasion to care for Haasini at least in the last few months of pregnancy. The younger woman, however, was stubborn enough to tell her mother that everything was under control and that Aadhi would always be there to take care of her. Her parents had not the slightest idea of all the drama at their daughter's place.

To confirm her fears, the dressing table went down. A series of shattering noises followed suit. He had broken the mirror!

She rushed towards the front door but stood still when she heard another loud thud.

What if he hurt himself? she thought. She was not sure if she should go back and check on him or go over to Ambica for help. But her knees went weak and she was not able to move. Her fingers failed to let go of the doorknob. Her gown was getting soaked in a sticky watery fluid. A sudden searing pain shot between her legs every few moments. Her back hurt as if a red-hot iron block was placed right on top of it.

"Don't do this to me, oh God!" Her painful shriek seemed to echo in every corner of the mansion. Her contractions were getting stronger by the second. She managed to reach the front porch and shouted out to Ambica as loud as she could. But there was no response. There was not enough will in her to go over to Ambica and wake her up either.

All the commotion in the drawing room broke Aadhi's violent trance. He snapped back to his human self and walked out of the room. He felt light-headed and totally drained of energy. It took another painful shriek from downstairs for him to realise that something was very wrong with Haasini. He ran down, covering two steps at a time. He doubled his pace when he saw his wife propped against the wall, smeared in tears, blood, and yellowish-brown fluid—she was giving birth!

The familiar sight of blood and gore upset him. Images of dead men, guns, and terror played out in his mind. To him, the agony she was experiencing was no different from that of his comrades on the battlefield.

I cannot let anything happen to her...I can't. He kept saying this to himself as if it were a sacred chant and he knelt down in front of her. He took one look at her dilation, got back up to kiss her, and hurried towards the door. "Don't you worry, *Kannama.* I'll go fetch Ambica." His face was flushed.

She lay there, trying to push the baby out with her rapidly ebbing strength. She had another violent contraction when Aadhi sprinted back towards her and narrowly avoided a collision with the half-open door.

He was panting and somehow managed to mask his fear and helplessness. "Ambica is not around. I have asked our ostler to bring in his wife as early as he can." It was difficult seeing his wife in so much pain. "Haasini, my love, look at me. I am here for you, alright? We are going to get through this together. Hold my hand and keep pushing."

Haasini faintly nodded and held his hand tight. She gathered all the strength that could be mustered in three painfully deep breaths and did exactly as Aadhi asked her to do.

Ten minutes passed but nothing happened. She broke down and wailed. "The baby is a month early. If something were to happen to our child, I cannot forgive myself," she said tearfully.

"You are stronger than anyone I have ever known. You took charge of the farmers' guild in my absence, put up with my tasteless behaviour all these days, and still managed to love me more than I deserved. I am sure you have passed on your strength to our child. Nothing can ever happen to the little one." His eyes were clouding up. "You must do this, Haasini. For the baby..."

* * *

The ostler's wife rushed in. She took one look at Haasini's bloodied gown and thought aloud, "That is a lot of blood!"

Two other women came running inside. They were armed with a set of bedsheets, a pair of scissors, and a bag full of cotton rags. It took one glance at the young woman in labour for one of the make-shift midwives to run to the kitchen and fetch a bowl of water while the other hurried towards Aadhi. She requested him to wait outside. But he wouldn't budge. Haasini screamed, "Let him be. I need him!"

They were initially hesitant to work in the presence of a man. But the urgency of the situation took over and they soon got down to business.

"*Thayi*, you are dilating well enough to be able to bring out your child in a few powerful pushes." Revathi soaked a piece of cloth in the bowl and dabbed Haasini's raging hot forehead.

A quarter of an hour passed by and yet the situation was not getting better. Without wasting any more time, the midwives sprang into action and methodically helped Revathi move her hands in the downward direction below Haasini's chest. Applying fundal pressure was not a favoured practice but they had seen enough deliveries to know that some women needed that extra push.

The sight of his wife suddenly becoming so vulnerable blinded Aadhi. Her clenched teeth and the way her tired body collapsed every time she tried was way more than his battle-hardened eyes were prepared to see. But the thought of battle reminded him of the most important lesson he had learnt: Fight only your enemy and not your pain. For you must feel the pain to stay alive.

Aadhi urged her to take a few deep breaths before another wave of agony overtook her. "Haasini, don't fight it. It's okay not to be in control. Just go with it and it will lead you through."

No one was sure if whatever happened next was a result of his encouragement or whether she did it because there was no other choice.

A Zen-like aura descended upon her and she closed her eyes for a brief moment. When she opened them, she saw a little boy seated at the other end of the room. His nose was every bit like Aadhi's. A gloomy expression hung over his face and he waved at her, as if to say, "Fare thee well." Before she could respond, he ran out the door and vanished into the dark.

"I guess this is it." Her voice cracked as she spoke.

Turning to her right, she watched the clock tick its way to two hours past midnight. Exactly eight minutes later, Siddhaman Aadhisankaran Chettiyar was born. He nestled in his mother's warmth while she slipped into delirium. Voices around her and the occasional shrill cries of her newborn son seemed like a distant echo. Her eyes lost focus and her pulse dropped. Exactly four hours past midnight, she went out through the door in search of the boy and never returned.

* * *

"Oh my God...you died right after giving birth to my grandfather?"

Haasini shrugged and stared at the train of people walking towards the temple's exit gate. She replied with nonchalance, "Yes. It was painful at first but then things got better. The more I got to see my baby boy, the more at peace I felt. Watching him grow up was literally the only thing that kept me occupied. I was not much into discovering the philosophies and truths of life and death. All I wanted was to be with my family." Her pauses were getting longer now. "Things changed when my husband died a year after Siddhaman married your grandmother. He stayed with me out here for no more than twenty-eight days. His body and soul had already endured enough to learn all that is there to be learnt."

Akshara reached out to hold her hand. But then remembered that it had evaporated and swiftly rested a gentle palm on her left knee. "How did you handle the pressure of such short-lived reunions and separations?"

"The unending cycle of life, separation, death, reunion and then again, separation pushed me to a breaking point. I finally gave up on my stubbornness and embraced the wisdom of death." She forcefully brought about a smile on her lips. "I felt especially blessed when the messenger souls taught me about the ultimate truth, just the way I taught Siddhaman, who in turn is teaching you." Haasini tried to pat Akshara's leg with her fast-disappearing right palm.

"Please don't mind me asking but Haasini, what happened to your husband after you died? Do you loathe him for what he had done to you?"

"Oh come on, *Kanna*...Don't you say that. I could not hate him in a thousand years. We did have a brief period of undeniable struggle but that never stopped me from loving him." Her nose wrinkled up as she smiled.

How could she be so forgiving...Akshara's thoughts fleeted in all directions. She felt a deep hatred towards her great-grandfather on one end and compassion on the other.

"Did your husband, my great-grandfather bring up grandpa all alone?" Akshara asked, preparing herself; she knew that the story of her ancestors was bound to break her heart into a million pieces.

Fading Away

15ᵗʰ November, 1949

While the country grappled with the realities of uniting the many princely states and struggled to raise a brood that was 360 million strong, Aadhi seated himself on a rusty chair and tried to soak in the sights of an unusually cold winter morning at Valimaioor. He was only fifty-nine but looked and felt as if he were ninety. He could no longer endure the chilly weather and decided to go back into his cottage. Inside, a bulky radio called for his immediate attention. It was two years since the British left, at least superficially. The excitement of Independence had almost died. Innocent people—the ones at home and in exile—died violent deaths. Communal riots had become so common that news readers no longer spoke more than a sentence about them. People woke up to the same old rooster's call and had the very same problems that plagued them and the society at large before. They had limited encouragement to tune in to the news. Multiple ideologies, events, and political blunders ripped an already maimed country apart and flung each of its pieces in a hundred different directions.

"Oh divine powers of heaven, this land has seen far too many trials and tribulations already. Bless the people with peace and contentment." He chanted a few mantras and joined hands as he prayed. A minute passed before he opened his eyes and looked out through the window.

A thin carpet of red phlox bloomed on either side of the stairs leading up to the porch. But except for a few colourful flowers here and there, the whole place oozed neglect. However, the stainless-steel coffee cup that he forgot outside shone amid all this gloom. And as surprising as it may seem, Aadhi too had found some warmth and colour on the other side of the street.

A young girl not older than eighteen had moved in with her family three months ago. He was amazed at how she reminded him of Haasini with the way she dressed and walked.

If we had a daughter, I am sure she would be just like her, Aadhi spoke in his mind and hoped that Haasini was listening. He yearned to speak with the two wonderful women but was unable to do so for two very different reasons. On the one hand, his wife was dead and unreachable while on the other, a young stranger was beginning to control his emotions while he sat there, hoping to be able to talk to her someday. It was a peculiar feeling.

Just like every other morning since she moved in, she placed a bunch of delicate blue and pink flowers on the square mahogany table. The light streaming in from the central French window added a regal touch to her villa and the breezy red sari that she wore multiplied her exuberance manifold. Rajeswari was young, intelligent, and full of life. She usually liked to spend most of her time outdoors but ever since she moved to this part of the city, finding friends was proving to be exceptionally difficult. All her peers in the locality were either already married or engaged. It was only the other day that she went over to visit Kamala who lived with her husband and in-laws, two houses away. But she regretted that her unmarried status became the talk of the evening. For Rajeswari, the odds of befriending the lonely old gentleman on the other side of the street seemed better than finding the comrades of her age. The temple bells rang while she contemplated the possibility of visiting him for the 100th time.

That's a good sign I guess, she thought to herself with a grain of confidence.

Twenty-nine years ago
15th November, 1920

Eleven-month-old Siddhaman was already awake. Aadhi had brought him to Rameswaram when he was only a month old. They had managed to secretly escape Valimaioor to ensure that none of Aadhi's family or friends knew where they were. In the first few months, most local newspapers had his photograph plastered in the Missing Persons' column. The story of Haasini's death spread like wildfire. Popular opinion was divided though. While some laid the blame on Aadhi, many others sympathised with him and even went out of their way, supporting him to stay incognito. His new beard and untamed hair helped him go about his new life, undetected...almost.

Things were relatively peaceful in Rameswaram. The salty waters on sun-kissed beaches washed away most of his grief and on that particular morning, it was especially beautiful. The baby woke up at 6.30 and was all smiles. He gurgled while excitedly looking towards the window. His eyes were wide with astonishment when he saw a bullock cart passing by. The sound of the bulls' hoofs as they moved in rhythm made him want to join them too. He moved his hips and did a peculiar half-squat dance that only babies can do.

"Morning, *Paiyaa*..." Aadhi cooed from the kitchen. The house was just one large chamber with a self-declared play area, bedroom, and drawing room, among others. He could see right across the room and smiled as his son danced and jumped in excitement while he was busy fixing up a scrumptious breakfast for the two of them. His baby was already comfortable eating solid food and had a special liking for soft finger-millet dosa.

Aadhi flipped the perfectly round, reddish-brown piece of culinary art and transferred it to a clay plate.

He hopped towards his son and started their favourite morning routine: Peek-a-boo. Siddhaman chuckled every time he discovered his father's loving face behind those big, masculine hands. Aadhi lifted his son in his arms and planted kisses on his chubby little cheeks. He carried his son over to the kitchen and handed him a glass of water. The child had mastered hand-mouth coordination when he was only eight months old and drank comfortably from a glass.

What followed was some playful finger-brushing and an hour-long breakfast session. A visit to the *Malikai Kadai* followed by a comfortable ride on his father's shoulders made Siddhaman the happiest child on earth. It was an especially comforting visit since the shopkeeper was rather friendly and even gave a packet of ginger toffees to the baby for free.

The villagers are finally accepting us into the community, Aadhi thought with great relief.

Back at home, he was filled with pride when Siddhaman successfully placed one building block over the other without faltering. The child's left hand supported the base structure as he tried to place another block on top. His motor skills and a refined sense of judgment took his cognitive skills months ahead of other babies his age.

Before they even realised it, it was 10 am already. Aadhi got busy preparing the baby's morning snack. Siddhaman had a glass of pomegranate juice only an hour ago but his fast-growing mind and body gave him the appetite of a lion and the energy of a rabbit.

While the baby sat in the company of his toys, Aadhi turned his face away from him and stole a quick moment to tidy up the place. Satisfied with his sparkling clean kitchen, he said, "Who wants a tasty snack?"

His heart skipped a beat when he realised that his son was not where he was just a few minutes ago.

"Siddhama?" he called out to him as he walked up to the mound of toys.

Gurgles greeted him from the open back door. Aadhi rushed out and found his little one casually walking towards the dirt road. An old lady from across the street had walked up to the infant. She was engaged in an animated conversation with him. The child giggled and continued walking while the lady kept a close watch.

Aadhi ran up to his son and picked him up. "Which eleven-month-old walks like this?" he was shivering with fear. A tight hug and a kiss on the forehead later, he spoke in awe of what his son had done. "You are such a special human...do you realise that?"

"*Thambi*, you need to keep a close watch on your kid. Now that he has started walking, he will bring in more trouble!" The old lady spoke as she walked back to her cottage. "Get married. The child needs a mother." She mumbled and sat under the neem tree in front of her humble home. Two other women her age joined her from the neighbourhood. Their mid-day gossip and analysis sessions had begun.

Aadhi thanked the lady, ignored her last comment, and carried his son back home. Up until then, he had not seen the child get up and move around even with support and was under the impression that the prospects of him walking were still a few months away.

They spent the next few minutes in the backyard as they walked back and forth; they were both eager to absorb the happy vibes around them. Just a few rounds into their newfound activity, a commotion on the dirt road brought them to a temporary stop. A few passers-by paused as well for a moment and observed a well-dressed young couple arguing with the village grocer. He was the same man who had handed Siddhaman his ginger toffee early that morning.

Anyone looking at the couple would know that they belonged to a well-to-do household. The man wore a crisp white *veshti* and a blue *khadi* shirt while the lady was dressed in a pink chiffon sari.

"I gave you hundred rupees already. How much more do you need?" The young man spoke out of frustration. Two days ago, he had received a call from this wretched shopkeeper who claimed to have information about Aadhi's whereabouts.

"Had I gone to the police, they would have rewarded me with three hundred rupees. Considering the reputation of your family, I approached you directly. And I am only asking for a hundred and seventy-five more." The grocer's greedy expression was too filthy to look at.

The young woman tugged at her companion and whispered something that made him look towards Aadhi, the baby, and the other people who stood around to watch the scene unfold. Without a word, he gave in to the man's demands and handed him the money he wanted.

"*Nanri, Ayya.*" The grocer smiled slyly. He motioned towards Aadhi and spoke in a sadistic tone. "Happy family reunion, *Anna.*"

As the two of them dismissed the grocer and walked towards the father-son duo, Aadhi instinctively picked the baby up and took a few steps back. He quickly walked into the house and closed the door.

The younger man ran up to the house but it was a bit too late. The door was already bolted.

"You cannot do this, Mama. You cannot run away anymore." He signalled his lady companion to walk up to the front door, just in case Aadhi was planning to do something crazy again.

"Open the door for God's sake. Let us not create a scene here." He became conscious of the many eyes that were boring into him from the houses nearby. He tried to ignore those people and went back to convincing Aadhi. There was no response.

Physically drained by the long journey and emotionally tired of everything that had taken place in the last year, he rested his forehead on the door and spoke in a defeated tone. "Mama, please open the door. Let us talk...I did not travel so far just to be greeted by a metal door." After a long pause, he measured his words and continued cautiously. "There is something you should know." His tongue was suddenly parched. Breaking such news was never easy. "Parvathy Aththai...she passed away a week ago. We had been trying really hard to get in touch with you." Raghavan paused and filled his lungs with a little more will to go on further. "She got very sick after you left."

He parted his lips to say something but before he could continue, his head jerked forward as the door opened. A teary-eyed Aadhi stood in front of him.

"What happened to my mother?"

"She took a fall and hit her head." Breaking such news was tougher than he thought.

Aadhi left the door open and walked back into the house. He started tending to the baby as if nothing had happened.

Raghavan called out for his wife and a few seconds later, they entered Aadhi's little abode together. There was silence because they did not know what to do. But their pent-up anger and disappointment was waiting to shred the silence to pieces. Surprisingly enough, Aadhi spoke.

"Only three days ago, I sent a letter to Amma along with a train ticket to Rameswaram. I was planning on introducing her to her grandson." He paused and waited for a lone drop of regret to fall from his left eyelid.

Raghavan's eyes were moist too. He shook his head and sniffled. Confident that his voice wouldn't crack, he whispered to his wife and broke the silence. "It's okay... you can go seek his blessings."

"There's no way I am going alone." She held his hand and dragged him along.

"Mama, meet Nalini, my wife. We got married when you were at the warfront. It was a very small wedding. We were fortunate to have had Parvathy Aththai's blessed presence."

"*Vanakkam, Anna.*" Nalini's voice was shaky with a tinge of nervousness. She joined her palms into a *Namaste* and bent down to touch Aadhi's feet. It was a mark of respect for his association with Haasini.

"I don't have the powers to bless you..." he felt lost as he helped Nalini up.

The young couple uncomfortably looked at each other and diverted their attention towards the baby.

"So, that's my little nephew…" Raghavan's face lit up as he walked towards the child.

"No…you can't do that." Aadhi blocked his way.

"He's my nephew and I have every right to do what I am about to do." He pushed his brother-in-law to the side and made his way to Siddhaman.

Aadhi was quick enough to regain control. He picked the baby in his arms and warned, "I know why you are here. This is my child and no one can take him away from me!"

"You cannot do this, you rotten piece of a man!" Raghavan spat out in anger. "Haasini was the gentlest of souls that had ever walked the planet. She cared for you…she loved you more than you deserved to be loved. It is a shame there was a point in time when I liked you. I idealised you. Hell! I wanted to be just like you…Glad I never succeeded with that!" A convulsive rage ran through his veins. "Is there any guarantee that you would not hurt this child the way you hurt my sister?"

Aadhi collapsed on the floor. Those words hit him hard. Siddhaman started crying at the sound of raised voices.

"Be thankful that we never filed a case against you or declared you mentally unfit. You should have been at the state asylum by now." Raghavan's eyes turned red. Soon enough though, he realised it was too harsh a statement. He no longer fought his tears and covered his face with his hands as his body shook in grief.

Nalini walked up to her husband and wrapped her arms around him. She had never seen him so deeply hurt. On the other side of the room, she saw another man who was drowning in his own helplessness.

Siddhaman sensed the tense atmosphere around him and started bawling. Nalini hastened towards his tiny bed and cradled him but he would not stop. She handed him the toy horse that she and Raghavan had brought along but nothing worked.

Raghavan collected himself, cleared his throat, and looked at Nalini. He motioned towards Aadhi and said, "That's fine, Nalini...take him over to his father." His voice was heavy after all that crying.

She hesitated a bit. Aadhi waited for her with a blank expression as she brought Siddhaman over to him.

As soon as he found the familiar comfort of his father's lap, the child stopped crying. He nestled against his chest and looked at the two confused strangers who stood in front of him as tears ran down their faces.

Siddhaman started crying again and Aadhi knew what was up. Without putting his son down, he raised himself towards the edge of the low table and reached for the bowl of boiled carrots and sweet potatoes he had prepared earlier. The little one dug straight in. He no longer needed his father to help him with his food. He was fast becoming an independent baby who knew how to use his fingers to feed his hair and clothes as well.

Redemption

16th November, 1920

Nalini was busy fixing a quick breakfast for the four of them. Events of the day before seemed as if a storm had hit them hard and then withdrew only to mend all that was broken. Aadhi found comfort in the familiarity of the family's presence and Raghavan found solace in having been reunited with his sister's husband. Nalini was unsure of how their visit would culminate.

The men were already seated on the floor and Siddhaman was keeping Raghavan busy. He was finally excited about his toy. Raghavan spoke to him as if he understood every bit of his baby talk. Aadhi felt a bittersweet joy as he saw the two of them bonding so well.

"Breakfast is ready," Nalini announced. "Please hold on to Siddhama. I'll bring in the dishes." Raghavan sat the child on his lap while his wife brought in piping-hot Idlis, Sambar, and Pongal. Satisfied with the arrangement, she served Aadhi on a large plate. "Here you go, Anna. The Dosas and chutney from last night were amazing. I am not as good a cook as you are. Please don't mind if the sambar tastes a little bland; I am still learning." She smiled nervously.

"This smells heavenly and tastes perfect." Aadhi smiled and reassured her. He stared at the plate and could not help but think about how he had messed up the lives of so many innocent people. Right from Haasini, to his mother, Raghavan, and now Nalini. These two youngsters should have been travelling for pleasure and not to a remote village to resolve a family dispute. They should have been romancing in the hills and beaches instead of visiting a troubled widower and his young son.

I must fix this...he thought with unbreakable determination.

As Nalini handed a plate over to Raghavan, she noticed that Siddhaman was now distracted from his horse. He was busy observing her. Even the previous day, after the initial spate of angry words and tears, the baby had watched her with great interest. Her heart melted as she looked at his beautiful, innocent face.

"Come on, Siddhama. Let's have breakfast." She spoke in a voice that was much sweeter than it usually was. Her smile was infectious and the child caught it faster than the others. Nalini extended her hands towards him and waited. A brief moment passed before the baby walked up to her without hesitation. He found a comfortable spot on her lap and ate while his doting aunt fed him from his favourite red-clay plate. The men looked at each other uncomfortably.

It is going to be painful for him if we take the baby away, Raghavan thought.

If only I could get enough strength to say goodbye to my son, Aadhi's heart and mind were at war with one another.

* * *

On 25th November 1920, when the auspicious full moon was sighted in the Tamil calendar month of *Karthigai,* Aadhi left his only son in the care of Raghavan and Nalini. They lived in urban Trichinopoly. Aadhi could wholeheartedly trust them. He even made plans to shift back to Trichy. Raghavan made sure that the father got to meet his son every Saturday. It was a tradition that was not broken till Aadhi breathed his last.

The Visitor

15ᵗʰ November, 1949

Three consecutive knocks on the door brought Aadhi back to the present. Taking a long walk down the road of memories and remorse had become a tradition of sorts for him in the mornings.

"Who would want me at seven a.m.?" he groaned. With unhurried, deliberate steps, he walked towards the corroded metal door. His bulky cane was slowing him down further.

The girl from the villa greeted Aadhi with a *vanakkam* as he stood near the door jamb.

"Good morning," she said and took a nervous pause. "Would you like to have some ginger tea and *masala vadai*?" she asked him. Her palms were sweating profusely.

"Of course, please come in," Aadhi ushered her in.

Anyone entering his tiny derelict habitat would undoubtedly notice the lone grilled window that bore the responsibility of shepherding in all the sunlight it possibly could.

He motioned towards an antique-looking tea table and pulled out a chair for her. When she was all settled, he seated himself on the other side of the table.

"Shall we?" asked the girl and placed three China cups, a thermos, and an oval stainless-steel box that filled the room with the aroma of freshly made masala *vadais*.

"I hope you are not finding this whole thing odd," Rajeswari was a lot more composed and even managed to sneak in a little smile while pouring tea into their respective cups.

"No, not at all. An old man like me can use a good cup of tea, especially in the company of someone as generous as you." He smiled and continued, "I am glad you are here."

"Won't your companion be joining us?" she asked.

"My companion?"

"Yeah, the one you talk to all the time."

"That would be my wife." He continued to sip his tea as if it were an elixir and paid no attention either to her questions or to his own replies.

"Where is she? Please ask her to join us."

"My wife is dead."

Her arched eyebrows and wide eyes gave away her bewilderment in an instant. For a moment, she began to doubt her decision to come over to him. He was an old stranger that she knew nothing about. She was tempted to run out of his dark habitat. Was that a haunted house? Or was he crazy?

"My apologies, *Chinnama*. I did not mean to be dramatic. My wife died during childbirth twenty-nine years ago… never got used to it though. I just like talking to her. Maybe, she is listening," he explained. The embarrassment on his face was quite evident.

"I am sorry for your loss, sir."

Aadhi nodded without uttering a word. An awkward silence followed.

"More tea?" she asked, trying to steer clear of the subject.

"No, thank you." He placed the cup on the table. "It has been ages since I had tea this good."

"I can bring tea every morning if you want." Rajeswari was beaming with anticipation.

"That is a very kind offer. But you don't want to upset your folks over an old man, do you?" He said in a husky voice.

"Oh, don't worry! I will take care of that." Her eyes were bright with excitement.

"But don't you have school?" he asked.

"I am done with school...will be pursuing a Bachelor's degree in Political Sciences at Queen Mary's. Classes commence in April."

"That is good to hear. My wife was one of the first few women to study there. Wonderful institution, I am told." He seemed highly impressed by her choice.

"She must have been a pioneer." The young woman was aware of the fact that going to college was a privilege for many women. The personal historical reference that Aadhi gave her made her want to pursue her college education with even greater zeal.

As she took pride in this newfound association with the past, a black and white wedding photograph of a young couple caught her attention. It was framed and hung a few inches above the table.

"Is that you, sir?" she pointed at the photograph.

Aadhi nodded. "And that's my wife."

The girl was awestruck. "She is beautiful. Why! That looks like my house!"

Nakshatra Illam made for a striking backdrop in the photo.

"I owned the place back in those days." He spoke as though there was nothing extraordinary about it.

"Why...why then would you live in this cottage?" she asked, perplexed.

"It was too big for me."

Who would want to let go of such a beautiful home? She could not put a stop to her thoughts. The villa was the largest and the most attractive building in the area. But for a few faded patches here and there, it was the kind of home that everyone dreamed of.

It took a while for her innocent mind to grasp the whole gravity of it. She was young and had little experience with regard to gauging and dealing with the complexities of adult emotions. However, that did not stop her from connecting with Aadhi. Probably her innocence allowed her to understand him better.

The roar of an approaching car drew their attention to the narrow pathway in front of the cottage.

"That must be Siddhaman," Aadhi announced as he walked up to the door. He was met by a young man in his late twenties. The girl noticed that he was a spitting image of the older gentleman. He looked exactly like Aadhi in the wedding photo, the one she had just seen a few minutes ago.

"Good morning, Appa. How are you doing today?" asked Siddhaman as he walked into the house.

"I have been well, *Kanna*," Aadhi replied. "I was getting a bit restless...feels like it has been ages since I saw you last."

"Oh come on, Appa, we only met last Saturday!" The youngster laughed and hugged Aadhi in a way that every son must hug his father. "Raghavan Mama and Nalini Aththai are looking forward to meeting you for dinner tomorrow."

"I will be there." The father was all smiles. "It is so good to see you. Come on in. We have a special guest."

The goodness of tea and *vadai* was tripled and the trio struck up an effortless conversation.

"I must thank you not just for all this delicious food but also for taking the time to visit my father." He took the last sip of tea from his cup and said, "Strange we have never met. So, I presume Mr. Swamy is your father?"

She nodded with a smile.

"Ah...thought so. I am Siddhaman by the way, his one and only son."

"I am Rajeswari and it is such a pleasure to meet you."

Siddhaman's heart skipped a beat when her almond eyes met his gaze. He realised that true to her name, her face was akin to that of the queen of goddesses. After six embarrassing seconds, he managed to speak. "You have a lovely name."

She smiled and the two struggled to keep their cheeks from turning red.

Aadhi was witnessing the inception of a relationship that would eventually culminate in marital bliss. The two of them blushed more and spoke less. At one point, they were both so overwhelmed by the rush of new, sweet feelings that they could not look each other in the eyes. Siddhaman was especially shy and chose to leave before he could give himself away.

"Miss, it was a pleasure talking to you. I am afraid I must leave." He bowed slightly and his palms touched to form a respectful *vanakkam.*

Rajeswari returned his courtesy ever so humbly. The deep red shade of her smiling lips shimmered as the sun shone upon her face.

Siddhaman feebly nodded. He had to get to the city to close a deal with a nationally recognised rice supplier. He also had to arrange for the farmers' representative meeting the next day. But then, as he traced his steps to the door, a wave of intense longing swept his logic away and he chose to forget all about his commitments. All he wanted to do was to stay back and sit by her side as she spoke in her chirpy voice. His father had to call him a couple of times before gaining his attention.

"Siddhama? *Kanna*...all okay?" Aadhi was pleased with the new development. But he chose to be the all-knowing father who tried really hard to act like he knew nothing. He wanted to play along just to have some fun. Watching his son fall so hard for someone was something he did not want to miss.

"Appa, did you say something?" Siddhaman wore a puzzled look.

"I was saying that maybe you could pick me up at six tomorrow evening."

"Yes, of course, Appa." He sat in the car and enquired, "Appa, I know we have spoken about this earlier but don't you think you should move in with me? It is kind of hard seeing you struggle out here. You even refused my proposal to hire a maid. Please Appa, let me care for you," he pleaded.

"Don't worry about me, Siddhama. I may not be as strong as you but I am certainly capable of taking care of myself. Moreover, you will need a reason to visit your new friend again...won't you?" He patted him on the shoulder and bid him an encouraging farewell. His son was all smiles as he drove off towards the city. Aadhi waited till the car moved out of sight before returning to his guest.

"My apologies, *Chinnamma*. I did not intend to keep you waiting for so long."

"Not at all, sir. In fact, I should be going too." Rajeswari picked up her bag and started walking towards the entrance. "See you tomorrow."

"Won't you be taking your tea cups?"

"That won't be necessary. Carrying the dishes every morning would be cumbersome, don't you think?" Her mischievous smile lit up the whole place. "Please call out if you need anything."

There was a sense of *déjà vu* that Aadhi could not brush away. She waved from the other side of the road and disappeared into the opulence of Nakshatra illam...

Farewell

"Our family couldn't be any more beautiful," Haasini spoke with an air of contentment.

Akshara's head was a whirlwind of emotions. "This has been..." tears choked her. It took enormous effort before she could continue, "this has been the greatest eye-opener, Haasini. I just..."

Haasini kissed her great-granddaughter on the cheek and hugged her with whatever little remained of her body. Everything else was shiny gold dust. The fine sprinkles swirled around her before evaporating above their heads.

"Oh my God! Your face is..." Akshara stopped midway to manage her runny nose.

"I think it is time for me to leave," Haasini spoke in a low-pitched quiver.

Akshara had gotten so attached to her in the last few hours that letting her go seemed like an impossible task. It was like she was seeing someone die afresh. A part of Haasini's face had already evaporated and so did her torso. All that remained was a section of her right eye, nose, lips and midriff; they too were soon turning into fine gold dust.

A sense of decisiveness descended upon Akshara as she announced, "I will go get Thatha then. He must want to meet his mother before she leaves..."

"Don't worry about that, *Kanna*. The messenger souls are already on their way to fetch him. He should be here any moment."

As if on cue, Thatha joined them.

"You are finally here..."

"Of course, I am, Akshara." A spontaneous hug followed. He looked at her face and breathed an air of satisfaction. "Your face is lit up with the brilliance of a thousand suns. Amma has indeed imparted the best of knowledge." His smile was still intact as he turned towards his mother, "All set, Amma?"

"Looks like it, little one..." Haasini spoke to her ninety-eight-year-old son. Her voice was eerily calm and peaceful. Just as her torso vanished, the messenger souls surrounded her. Their tranquil voices sang in a beautiful chorus. Their words, however, were not words at all. A gentle breeze flowed towards the congregation and in one big swirl, swept away all of Haasini's gold dust. She was gone. All that remained was her voice. She had officially become a messenger soul.

Akshara squeezed Thatha's right arm as she stood next to him. "Is that how they speak?"

He nodded in agreement. "That is how they speak, Akshara. Words hold no meaning for them. The primordial sounds of the universe are all they use."

"That's strange. How then was I able to understand what they sang?" she paused for a moment and looked towards him, feeling confused. "I mean I know I understood them. But if you ask me to explain, I am unable to!" Her mouth was still half open. "Why?"

"They were the sounds of the beginning, the end, and everything in-between. Don't worry about wanting to explain. Certain things do not need to be explained." His eyes were moist. "I am so proud of you, *Kanna*." He wrapped his left arm around her shoulder. "It's time for you to leave as well."

"Thatha?"

"It is time for you to go back to life."

"So soon?" Akshara did not want to listen to anything further. How could she leave him behind and just go away?

"Don't you want to go back?" he asked.

"I want to...but I also don't want to go." She slumped to the ground and held her head with both hands. "I just don't know, Thatha. I don't know what to do..."

"Oh dear child, that is precisely why you must go back. You are still not ready to get over the bonds of attachment. This is a sign! Your body needs you, Akshara." He sat next to her and clutched her hand tightly. "When I died, I so badly wanted to get back to my body. I wanted to be alive...to be well. I wanted to be around to see my youngest grandchildren grow up, to see you get married." There was a pause as the two of them fathomed the depths of his words.

"Even now, if given a chance, I would gladly embrace life and get back to being alive. I probably came out as being too confident and happy in this place when we spoke earlier yesterday." His hands were slightly shaky as he spoke. He seemed as fragile as he did on his deathbed. Akshara could not hold back her tears any further.

"You see, I have no choice, *Kanna*. And I had none back then either. My body had lived up to the ripe old age of ninety-eight." He ruffled her hair and spoke earnestly, "But you are still young. It is true that your body is hurting now but it has the power to heal. You must go back."

Akshara leaned on her grand old man. Her head rested on his shoulder as she spoke in a feeble voice. "But then, you will be all alone. Even Haasini is not here anymore. Who will keep you company?"

"Oh well... don't worry! Kandasamy will keep me company. Moreover, I must train myself to get over everything and everyone to finally move ahead to the next stage...don't you agree?" His eyes wore a glint of hope. "The messenger souls are going to guide you through the whole process. Just follow their lead and don't forget to breathe."

Mild breezy waves touched Akshara's face and the voices sang in cosmic chorus once again. They looked around with anticipation.

"Do I have time to ask you one last question, Thatha?"

He spontaneously engulfed her in the warmth of his wrinkled arms. "Of course."

"Do you remember, Thatha, I visited you at the hospital just a day before you passed away?"

"I do, yes."

"I felt as if you were trying to say something. But the tubes got in the way. You were too weak to even speak... What was it?"

"Glad you reminded me of that. I wanted to tell you that I met my mother. I wanted to tell you about this dimension of existence. Just like you, I too kept oscillating between life and death. It was such a scary yet exhilarating experience, to say the least. I had to share it with someone but bad luck, there was not an ounce of energy left in me."

The voices of the messenger souls got a bit louder as she prepared to bid him farewell. "Will I ever see you again?"

"I hope not. I hope you live a very long, happy life." Thatha squeezed her hand one last time and let go of it before she could reciprocate.

Sparks

19th July, 2015

The light was blinding and the sound deafening. Everything was blurry-white. Her body felt heavy and numb to the core.

"Hello there, little one." A familiar voice greeted Akshara.

She had to know what was happening and squeezed her eyes open to get a clearer view. It was a frustrating experience, to say the least. Even after a good many attempts, her vision was a hazy mess. All she saw was a blurry old woman in a sari. Even as Akshara tried to get a clearer view of her face, the woman's jet-black kohl-lined eyes caught her attention.

"Rajeswari Paati…" Akshara's voice was faint.

"I am right here. Thank heavens…you are going to get better in no time." She wiped tears off her face and pressed her granddaughter's arm ever so gently.

"Amma and Appa?" Akshara's thoughts and words were slow.

"They just left to catch up on some sleep. Your parents were here three days in a row." Rajeswari Paati's smile was brimming with grandmotherly love. "I am not leaving your side. Don't you worry about a thing."

Akshara tried hard to listen to everything her grandma said and closed her eyes in drowsy contentment. Eyes still closed, she tapped her Paati's hand and said, "Thatha is doing fine. He has become more energetic now. And his mother Haasini is such a beautiful, intelligent woman. I totally fell in love with her. She also told me about the wonderful tea and *vadais* that you carried over to great-grandpa Aadhi's place."

Akshara blinked again in an attempt to see Paati's reaction through a layer of invisible glue in front of her eyes. "Sorry...I've never talked to you about your past...your life. But now that I know a lot about you and Siddhaman Thatha, things are going to be different." There was so much more for her to speak but the invisible eye glue became even stronger. Without any further strength to fight it, Akshara just closed her eyes, inhaled, and said, "Love you, Paati..."

www.ingramcontent.com/pod-product-compliance
Lightning Source LLC
Chambersburg PA
CBHW021224130726
47988CB00002B/811